Dead Line: Midnight

It's a quarter-to-death and Schuyler Harlew is about to meet his maker. The bell will toll for him as the clock strikes twelve and an unseen hand takes yet another life as if by mutual consent. For Schuyler Harlew knows his killer—and he is as ready as he will ever be for his appointment with death. Harlew is Number One, the first in a long line of inventors to die; the first to leave a posthumous clue to the killer's identity—three extended fingers, a loosely circled fist and crossed wrists: M-O-X. It is The Shadow's only lead to an arch-fiend who is also a master of disguise and a devastating connoisseur of the art of crime. Mox, the man of many faces, boldly declares, "Murder is my living."

Who is Mox? How can his epidemic of evil be stopped?

The Shadow Knows!

Also published by Pyramid Books:

THE LIVING SHADOW—SHADOW #1
THE BLACK MASTER—SHADOW #2
MOBSMEN ON THE SPOT—SHADOW #3
HANDS IN THE DARK—SHADOW #4
DOUBLE Z—SHADOW #5
THE CRIME CULT—SHADOW #6
THE RED MENACE—SHADOW #7

MOX

FROM THE SHADOW'S PRIVATE ANNALS

as told to

MAXWELL GRANT

PYRAMID BOOK ▲ NEW YORK

MOX
A PYRAMID BOOK

Published by arrangement with The Conde Nast Publications Inc.

Pyramid edition published September 1975

Originally published in SHADOW Magazine, Volume VII, Number 6,
November 1933

ISBN 0-515-03876-8

Printed in the United States of America

Pyramid Books are published by Pyramid Communications, Inc.
Its trademarks, consisting of the word "Pyramid" and the portrayal
of a pyramid, are registered in the United States Patent Office.

Pyramid Communications, Inc., 919 Third Avenue,
New York, N.Y. 10022

CONTENTS

I.	THE DEADLINE	7
II.	MURDER DISCOVERED	12
III.	THE INVESTIGATION	19
IV.	THE BROKEN TRAIL	26
V.	THE STROKE OF TWELVE	32
VI.	THE SHADOW MOVES	37
VII.	TRAILS CONVERGE	41
VIII.	IN THE HOUSE	47
IX.	CARDONA TAKES A TRIP	55
X.	THE SECRET ROOMS	61
XI.	WEIRD VISITORS	68
XII.	CARDONA DRAWS A TRUMP	73
XIII.	THARBEL COUNTERS	77
XIV.	THE SHADOW ENTERS	82
XV.	THE TEST	85
XVI.	CARDONA'S TEST	92
XVII.	DEATH INTERRUPTS	96
XVIII.	DEATH RETURNED	102
XIX.	CARDONA'S PLAN	109
XX.	BEFORE MIDNIGHT	114
XXI.	THE FATAL HOUR	118
XXII.	DOOM DEFERRED	121
XXIII.	CARDONA LEARNS	124

Chapter I

THE DEADLINE

The green glass shade of the desk lamp threw a greenish, ghoulish glare upon the man who was seated at the desk. A twitching face betrayed the nervous thoughts of the man, a trembling hand that clutched a pen showed the fear that dominated his actions.

With shaky, fitful effort, the man placed the point of the pen upon a long sheet of lined yellow paper. As he leaned toward the desk, his face showed more plainly in the light.

It was a pointed face—a peaked countenance that betokened a glib, persuasive talker. Under the present circumstances, however, terror alone was registered upon that pale-hued visage.

A clock was ticking on the desk. Set on a swivel, it was turned slightly upward, so the man could watch it as he wrote. The clock marked the time as ten minutes before midnight. Glancing from paper to clock and back again, the man inscribed these words:

Statement of Schuyler Harlew.

A pause. Schuyler Harlew leaned back in his chair, aghast. His expression was that of a man who had taken an irretrievable step. A short, fearful gasp came from Harlew's lips, as though he expected the very walls of the room to collapse about him. He threw a worried glance in every direction.

The room was small and plainly furnished. The door was locked. The solid transom was closed above it. A high window, one of a pair which swung inward on hinges, was partly opened, so a slight draft came upon Harlew's right shoulder.

As he turned about in his chair, Harlew leaned toward the window. He rose slightly to reach the level of the sill. He listened intently, then peered out into the night.

Blackness dominated the vicinity. The room, three stories up, was above the level of the low houses on the other side of the street. In the distance, beyond the area of taller houses several blocks away, hung the dull glow of a great metropolis.

To any one familiar with New York City, that illumination and the direction from which it appeared, would have been sufficient to locate the spot where Schuyler Harlew was now situated. The house which contained this little room was located somewhere in the upper section of New York City—the Bronx.

Satisfied that no strange sound from outside might be a warning, Schuyler Harlew turned back to his desk. He held the pen more firmly. Beneath the line which revealed his name he wrote these startling words:

To be delivered to The Shadow.

As before, Harlew rested back in his chair. On this occasion, his lips ceased twitching. Their restlessness was replaced with a smile of satisfaction. The writing of that name, The Shadow, brought confidence to the nervous man.

The Shadow!

Known everywhere as a superbeing, who battled against fiends of crime, he was one to whom those who knew of evil deeds could turn. A grim avenger, who stalked forth upon his missions enshrouded by night itself, The Shadow was always prepared to throw his might in favor of those whom danger threatened.

No one knew The Shadow's real identity. No one knew where The Shadow could be reached. But Schuyler Harlew seemed satisfied that The Shadow, with all the power at his command, would certainly learn of this message, should it fall into the hands of any other than enemies.

Why not? Everything seemed possible to The Shadow. Millions knew his voice, for it had been broadcast. His exploits were legend. His raconteur had told the world of amazing episodes in the career of this master battler against crime.

Criminologists had stated that The Shadow, marvel of darkness, was, in himself, the great controlling agent who entered the endless war between crime and justice. When the depredations of evildoers seemed to outweigh the

8

strength of the police, The Shadow was invariably thrust into the balance, upon the side of the law.

The Shadow might be anywhere; at times, he seemed to be everywhere. He scented crime of insidious purpose with the instinct of a bloodhound. He arrived at scenes where crime threatened with the speed of a hurricane. He struck with the power of a giant. A lone wolf who battled crime, his hand never failed.

Schuyler Harlew had considered these facts. To him, as he began to write, it seemed positive that the message would reach The Shadow. Imbued with confidence, Harlew began a rapid scrawl underneath the heading of his statement.

Death threatens me. I know that death has been the lot of others. I know that death will continue. I have been a fool. I have aided a monster in his schemes of death.

Harlew paused. His lips began to twitch. His eyes, steadying upon the words that his hand had written, saw the name of The Shadow emblazoned on the paper. Harlew's hand steadied.

Midnight is the hour that the monster chooses. At midnight, he has talked with me. He has given me instructions and the time that I must return. I obeyed him in the past. I always returned to his hidden abode until one day ago; then I gained courage. I did not keep my appointment with my fiendish master.

The little clock on the desk showed five minutes before twelve. Harlew's teeth grated with determination. Feverishly, he resumed his writing.

To fail in my appointment with this evil master held one penalty—doom. Sure doom, within twenty-four hours after such failure. I have risked my life. I have hidden. Less than five minutes remain before midnight. Once that deadline is passed, I shall be safe—for I shall know that the fiend has not found my hiding place.

I have been afraid to write my statement. I have begun now that I may be finished, when midnight comes. I dare not betray him until I am sure of safety.

9

As soon as my little clock tells me that midnight has passed, I shall write the monster's name.

Then I shall post this letter—or leave it here— which, I cannot decide. I can think more sanely, once I know that I am free. This letter must reach the one to whom I have addressed it. He, alone, can meet and defeat the monster. Once I am safe, I shall flee.

The clock showed one minute before twelve. Its measurement of time was precise; for it had a little second hand which was just starting on the final minute. Watching the clock, Harlew wrote mechanically—he inscribed an involuntary thought upon the paper:

One minute: then the name:

Pen poised in hand, Harlew watched the second hand mark off its tiny portions of time. Each second seemed endless to this man who had forgotten all else in his anxiety to make sure that he would escape the doom he feared.

Fifteen seconds; twenty. Harlew was a living statue. His eyes were bulging as they stared at the clock. His breath came in long, inaudible puffs.

Thirty seconds. Harlew remained rigid. He was fascinated by the slow upward journey of the tiny pointer that seemed to hold its course while life lay in the balance.

At fifteen seconds before twelve, an involuntary trembling caught Harlew's frame. At ten seconds before the hour, the shaking had increased to a palsy.

Five seconds to go. Harlew's face was twitching in fierce contortions. Four seconds; three; two; one—the pointer of the second hand reached the high spot, just as the minute and hour hands together formed an upright bar directly to the number twelve.

Midnight! The deadline!

To Schuyler Harlew, all hope clung to that single, lingering moment. Every hand of the clock seemed immobile; even the pointer that showed the seconds seemed reluctant to budge a hair's breadth from its position.

Then Harlew's eyes saw space. The second hand had moved. As a gasp came from the maddened man's lips, the pointer seemed to swing downward in a merry, care-free journey, like a motor car that had labored over the crest of a terrific hill.

The deadline had been passed! The clock showed it!

Shrieks of laughter came from Harlew's lips. He was gleeful as he watched the friendly second hand, clicking off bits of time which now seemed released. Five seconds; ten seconds; fifteen——

Hunching upward in his chair, Harlew arose with the air of a man about to sign a momentous document. He was holding the pen firmly; although his wrist seemed weak, it was through joy, not fear. Placing his left hand on the sheet of yellow paper, Harlew jabbed the pen point downward.

A dab of ink upon the paper. That was all. A wild gasp came from Harlew's lips, the sound of sudden anguish. The man's stooped body straightened upward. The pen dropped from Harlew's helpless hand. It clicked against the face of the clock, which now marked twenty seconds past midnight.

Harlew threw his hands toward his back. His fingers clawed helplessly. The stricken man circled as he staggered toward the door. Desperately, he clutched at the key; it came loose from the lock and fell. Harlew swayed. His legs collapsed. He sprawled headlong upon the floor, arms in front of him.

His hands reached weakly as though they sought the pen which lay upon the desk. Harlew tried to gasp a name.

With a final effort, he brought his left hand flat to the floor, one finger—the little one—doubling underneath the palm. His right hand thudded as it formed a loose fist. With an effort, Harlew brought it up and down; this time, across his left wrist.

From that instant, Schuyler Harlew did not move again. Protruding from the center of his back was the instrument that had caused his death—a long, thin-bladed knife, pointed like an ice pick, with a cylindrical handle no thicker than a spool of cotton thread.

As the last gasp came from Harlew's bloated lips, the little clock upon the desk told the time that death had taken. The long hand had reached one minute after midnight. The tiny indicator had clicked off ten seconds more, on another downward run.

Like a knell for the man who had met his doom came a distant, booming chime. Its dongs resounded in slow, funereal tone, as though they, not the knife blade, had been responsible for the end of Schuyler Harlew.

One—two—three—the strokes continued. The final toll ended the count of twelve. That distant clock, accurately

11

set, had marked the midnight hour. It also, on this night, signaled the deadline which Schuyler Harlew had feared. It told the limit of the time which the threatening fiend had given to the man who had planned to betray him.

Schuyler Harlew was dead, his body contorted, his hands and arms in a peculiar twist. The yellow paper, Harlew's message to The Shadow, still rested on the desk. Beyond it was the little clock which had played so great a part in Harlew's hopes and fears.

The little timepiece ticked on and on, the only object that seemed alive within this room of death. Schuyler Harlew had set it only a few days before. He had supposed then that its time was accurate.

In that supposition he had been wrong. Thus had his actions been guided by a false belief. The booming tones of the distant chime had tolled the solemn truth.

The little clock on Schuyler Harlew's desk was seventy seconds fast!

CHAPTER II

MURDER DISCOVERED

It was early the next evening. At headquarters, Detective Joe Cardona was seated alone at a desk. Cardona, known as an ace detective, was at present in a special capacity. He was Acting Inspector Cardona, serving in place of Inspector Timothy Klein, who was confined to his home by illness.

There was one thing which both rankled and pleased Cardona. Since Inspector Klein had gained a state of convalescence, it was Joe's duty to report constantly to his superior. The acting inspector had no reason to resent this condition that had been imposed upon him; indeed, Cardona would have willingly kept Klein informed of the details which took place at police headquarters.

But Cardona had a hunch that Police Commissioner Ralph Weston, through visits to Inspector Klein, was keeping tabs on what Cardona was doing. This was why Cardona felt uneasy. He knew that he rated high with Weston; at

12

the same time, he felt an inferiority complex so far as the commissioner was concerned.

Weston—to use Cardona's own mental phraseology—had the "Indian sign" on the star detective. A keen, dynamic sort of man, the police commissioner had more than once expressed the opinion that Cardona relied too much on hunches. So far as Weston was concerned, Cardona preferred to let him judge by results rather than by actual observation of Cardona's working methods.

The tingle of the telephone bell presaged something important. Cardona lifted the receiver, grunted a hello, and began to make notations on a slip of paper as he listened. His hieroglyphics recorded, Cardona hung up the receiver. He waited a few minutes, then, with a grim look, went back to the telephone and called Inspector Klein.

"Just got a call from Mowry's precinct," informed Cardona. "Murder up there. Man dead in a rooming house in the Bronx. Told them to hold everything until I got up there."

"Unusual circumstances?" queried Klein's voice.

"Yeah," returned Cardona. "Guy stabbed in the back; third-floor front room. No way anybody could have got into the place, and out again. Besides that——"

Cardona paused thoughtfully. Klein's voice came promptly over the wire.

"Well," added Acting Inspector Cardona, "the guy left a note. I want to see it. May be something important. It's addressed to The Shadow——"

"To The Shadow?" Klein's question was a surprised echo.

"Yeah," admitted Cardona, "to The Shadow. So they told me from the precinct. I'll call you after I get up there, inspector."

Cardona hung up the receiver with a bang. He was angry; and with reason. He could see trouble when this news reached Commissioner Weston.

Joe Cardona, during his career as detective, had seen positive proof of The Shadow's prowess. In fact, Joe owed his life—not once, but several times—to The Shadow's intervention.

Yet always, Joe had seen The Shadow only as a mysterious being, garbed in black, or in a disguise that veiled his true features.

The mention of such a personage in Cardona's reports

13

had aroused the ire of Commissioner Weston. According to the commissioner, The Shadow—until he could be given a more tangible identity—must be regarded as nothing more than a myth.

A letter to The Shadow!

If such a note were important, it would be best to let it reach The Shadow somehow. But to give it to reporters would be a great mistake. Commissioner Weston's antagonism would be aroused. Reporters, to Cardona, were both bane and blessing. He hated their interference; he liked their commendation, when it appeared in print.

Looking toward the door, Cardona found an answer to his very thoughts. Smiling from the frame of the doorway was a young man about thirty years of age, light in weight, and almost frail in build, but whose face showed both experience and determination. Cardona recognized Clyde Burke, reporter of the New York *Classic*.

"Hello, inspector," greeted Burke, with a friendly wave of his arm.

"Lay off that inspector stuff," growled Cardona. "I'm Detective Cardona—Joe to you."

Rising as he spoke, the detective faced the reporter. There was a contrast between the two. Burke's face was tapering; his blue eyes and frank smile were disarming. Cardona, with square jaw, swarthy countenance, and glowering eyes of deep brown, was harsh and outspoken. Forty pounds heavier than Burke, though the two were of a height, Cardona showed a challenge as he stepped toward the reporter.

"Did you hear me talking on the telephone?" he demanded.

"Couldn't help it, Joe," returned Burke.

"What did you hear me say?"

"Something about a murder up in the Bronx . A letter in his room. Addressed to The Shadow——"

"Yeah?" Cardona's fists clenched, then opened. "Well, Burke, you're a good egg. I asked you what you heard, and you told me. You couldn't have heard anything else, because that's all I said."

"What of it, Joe?" queried Burke. "I'm a friend of yours. All I want is the story—if it's a good one—the way you give it to me."

"O.K., Burke," growled Cardona. "You're one news chaser that I can count on. Listen. I don't want this to go out until I've been there. I'm going up to the Bronx, but

I'm not taking you with me. If you blow in of your own accord, all right. Here's the address; you could probably get it up at Mowry's precinct anyway.

"But this Shadow business is out. Understand? They're holding everything until I show up. When I give out a statement, The Shadow may be out of it. I don't want anything getting in the *Classic* that I haven't handed to you. The commissioner has been calling Inspector Klein; maybe he'll be calling him to-night. There are some things I've got to be cagy about. This is one of them."

"I understand, Joe," nodded Burke. "Leave it to me. I won't give the office anything until after you've looked over the lay. I'll just call them and tell them I'm going to the Bronx. Count on me, Joe."

The reporter sauntered from the office as Cardona prepared for his trip to the northern section of the city. Outside of headquarters, Burke entered a cigar store, and went into a telephone booth. He called a number.

A quiet voice answered him. It was not the voice of the man at the city desk in the *Classic* office. It was a voice, however, that Burke expected to hear. Over the wire came this statement:

"Burbank speaking."

"Burke reporting," returned Clyde in a cautious tone. "Murder in the Bronx. Dead man left a message to The Shadow."

"Continue with details."

Clyde tersely told all that he had gleaned from Joe Cardona. His report finished, the young man hung up and walked from the cigar store. He headed for the nearest subway station to begin his ride to the address where murder had fallen. He intended to be there—as reporter for the *Classic*—when Joe Cardona arrived.

Yet Burke had another purpose. He was anxious to see that letter, even though he would not print it in the *Classic*. For Clyde Burke's call to the quiet-voiced man named Burbank was of more importance than any news which might be gained for the columns of a newspaper. Clyde realized that as he walked along the street.

Clyde Burke was an agent of The Shadow. Veiling his operations by his connection with the *Classic,* Clyde was always on the lookout for situations such as the one which had just arisen. Burbank, the man whom Clyde had just called, was The Shadow's contact agent.

Through Burbank, The Shadow could be quickly reached. The mysterious master who battled crime was always in communication with Burbank. Thus Clyde Burke's statement regarding a dead man's message to The Shadow was already on its way to the one person who would find it most important: The Shadow, himself!

The quickness of The Shadow's system was evidenced by activities which Clyde Burke could not witness. In a small, secluded room, a man was seated at a lighted table. He was wearing ear phones; a lighted switchboard was set before him. The man's back was toward the darkened room. This was Burbank, contact agent for The Shadow.

Burbank pressed a switch. A light glowed. There was no response. Burbank pulled out the plug. He had just made a connection over a private wire to The Shadow's sanctum, the mysterious abode where The Shadow spent many secret hours. The lack of response showed that The Shadow had left the sanctum.

Methodically, Burbank made a regular telephone connection and dialed a number. There was a reply. A speaker announced that this was the Cobalt Club. Burbank inquired for Mr. Lamont Cranston. Shortly afterward, an even voice came over the wire:

"Hello. This is Mr. Cranston."

"Burbank speaking," declared The Shadow's agent.

"Report," came Cranston's voice.

Burbank relayed Clyde Burke's message. Quietly and methodically, he conveyed its entire substance. The reply was a final tone:

"Report received."

At the Cobalt Club, Lamont Cranston stepped from a telephone booth and appeared in the lobby. He was a tall man, with firm, well-chiseled features. There was something about his face—its inflexibility, perhaps—that made it appear like a mask superimposed upon the countenance beneath.

Known at the Cobalt Club as a multi-millionaire globe-trotter, Lamont Cranston was a notable member. The Cobalt was one of the most exclusive clubs in New York; to hold prestige there was a sign of real social importance.

Attired in immaculate evening clothes, Lamont Cranston formed an imposing figure as he stood in silent meditation. A thin smile had appeared upon his carven lips, his eyes seemed to burn as they stared toward the outer doorway. The most remarkable feature of this distinctive person was—strangely—his shadow.

Where Cranston's form eclipsed the light from the floor, a long shade appeared. Jet black in hue, it lay in clear-cut outline; a grotesque shape that terminated in a perfect silhouette!

That splotch of blackness was a symbol. It marked the true identity of this tall personage.

Lamont Cranston was The Shadow!

Within a dozen minutes after Clyde Burke had gleaned important information for his chief, almost before Joe Cardona, in his role of acting inspector, had started for the Bronx, The Shadow was acquainted with the fact that an unknown dead man had left a message for his perusal.

In the part that he was playing—that of Lamont Cranston, gentleman of leisure—The Shadow showed none of the swiftness which so characterized his usual actions when crime was in the wind. Club members, passing through the hotel lobby, nodded in greeting to Lamont Cranston, as the tall millionaire stood puffing a cigarette in apparent unconcern. It seemed that Cranston had an appointment with someone, and intended to keep it.

A man of pompous bearing strode into the lobby of the Cobalt Club. His shoulders were erect, his arms were swinging in a somewhat military manner. The doorman spoke and bowed. The newcomer glanced about the lobby in a rather brusque fashion. He noted Lamont Cranston. His face lighted and a smile appeared upon his dominating face.

"Ah!" exclaimed the arrival. "Sorry to keep you waiting, Mr. Cranston! I was detained at my office; in fact, I found it necessary to leave word that I could be reached here while dining with you."

"So I supposed," returned Cranston, with a quiet smile.

"How so?" inquired the arrival, in a tone of surprise.

"Because," said Cranston, "there was a call for you. I answered it. I managed to get the gist of it, commissioner."

The last word revealed the identity of the newcomer. This man, who had arrived to dine with Lamont Cranston, was none other than Police Commissioner Ralph Weston!

"A call!" interjected the commissioner. "In reference to——"

"To a murder," interposed Cranston, in his easy manner. "It appeared to be from a police inspector—from his home—the name slips me——"

"Klein?"

"Ah, yes. Inspector Klein. He has received a report from an acting inspector—I believe the name is Cardona——"

"Yes. Cardona." Weston was impatient.

"Cardona has started to a house in the Bronx." Cranston drew a slip of paper from his pocket. "This address, commissioner. A man was murdered there, it appears. Cardona is going to investigate. Inspector Klein seemed anxious that you should be there also."

Weston snatched the paper and studied it. A doubtful expression appeared upon his face. With a penchant for crime solution, he was anxious to find a way of postponing this dinner engagement with Lamont Cranston. The multimillionaire supplied the answer.

"So I arranged," remarked Cranston, "to have my limousine available. It is outside. I should be glad to ride with you to the Bronx if you feel that our dinner might best be postponed."

"Excellent," declared Weston warmly. "I shall accept your invitation. Let us go at once."

Lamont Cranston called for hat and coat. With Commissioner Weston, the millionaire strode from the Cobalt Club. A limousine drew up to the curb. They stepped in.

Commissioner Weston was elated at this turn of events. A showman by nature, a man who regarded his office as a unique position, Weston was pleased at the opportunity to take along so unusual a companion as Lamont Cranston.

The millionaire, in turn, wore a placid smile that Weston did not detect. The police commissioner had no inkling whatever to Lamont Cranston's real purpose in extending this invitation. He did not know that the supposed telephone message from Inspector Klein was a mere pretext.

Weston thought that Lamont Cranston was serving him. The contrary was the case. Weston was serving Lamont Cranston. In his guise of an influential millionaire, The Shadow was traveling to find the message which Schuyler Harlew had left for him.

The Shadow's passport on this unusual mission was the police commissioner of New York City!

CHAPTER III

THE INVESTIGATION

"Here's the body, inspector."

Joe Cardona grunted his response to the policeman who spoke the words. The officer had just swung open the door of the third-floor room. Cardona was staring at the form of Schuyler Harlew, spread upon the floor.

"We haven't touched anything," declared the policeman. "There's the letter on the table."

"All right," growled Cardona. "Captain Mowry told me all about it. He'll be up here in a minute."

A heavy man in the uniform of a police captain came up the stairs a few moments after Cardona had spoken. He stopped at the door beside the detective, and stood silently while Cardona studied the body. This was Captain Mowry, in charge of the precinct where the murder had taken place.

Cardona entered the room. He noted the light still burning in the green-shaded lamp. He saw the little desk clock. He observed the note that lay on the desk. He began to read it.

He was reaching forward to pick up the paper when he heard the sound of new footsteps on the stairs. He swung inquiringly toward the captain.

"I left word no one was to come up," announced the police officer. "Go ahead; I'll see who it is."

As the captain looked down the hall, Cardona stepped to the door. He saw the captain salute and step back a pace.

Peering from the room, Cardona saw the reason. The star detective repressed a scowl as he recognized Police Commissioner Ralph Weston.

"Hello, Cardona," was the commissioner's greeting. "Just heard from Inspector Klein that you were up here. You have met Mr. Cranston?"

Cardona nodded. He had met the prominent millionaire, and knew Cranston as a friend of Weston's. Cardona submitted to the commissioner's intervention with good grace. It paid to be friendly with Weston, as Cardona had learned, and now that the commissioner was here, there was nothing to do but accept the fact.

"Go right ahead, Cardona," ordered Weston. "Don't let us disturb you. Mr. Cranston and I are here purely as interested spectators."

Cardona resumed his study of the body. He received a sheet of notes from the captain. He referred to them as he crossed the room, and peered through the narrow space of the window.

Carefully noting the exact position of the hinged sash, he opened it farther and thrust his head through. He peered down a sheer wall three stories to the street. Withdrawing his head, he closed the sash part way to its original position.

He went to the desk, read the page of notes that he held, then picked up the yellow sheet upon which Schuyler Harlew had written. Turning to Commissioner Weston, Cardona made his statement.

"This man was living here under an assumed name," he said. "He called himself David Gurgler. His real name, according to this statement that he left, is Schuyler Harlew."

"When was he murdered?" inquired Weston.

"He had been staying here for three days," announced Cardona. "He was paid up for a week in advance. He called down the stairs for his meals; they were brought up to him. To-day, the landlady supposed that he had gone out for lunch. When dinner time arrived, she knocked at the door. It was locked. Harlew did not answer.

"The landlady—Mrs. Parsons—called for the police. The door was opened with a pass-key. Harlew was presumably slain last night. If this note is reliable, we can set the time at midnight."

Cardona handed the note to Weston. The commissioner, holding the paper so that Cranston could see it, began to read. He stopped upon the second line. As Cardona had expected, an angry look appeared upon Weston's face.

"Is this a hoax?" demanded the commissioner.

"I don't know, sir," responded Cardona. "I was informed at headquarters that the note was here on the desk. I was just reading it when you arrived."

20

"Hm-m-m," commented Weston. "The Shadow. Any document that refers to an imaginary being is worthless. If this man"—he pointed to Harlew's body—"wrote the note, he was probably in a frenzied, irrational condition. If some one else wrote it, and placed it here, we can regard the message as a hoax."

The commissioner continued to study the yellow paper, reading it over and over with an angry glare. Lamont Cranston, standing at Weston's elbow, had carefully perused every word. The millionaire was studying Cardona, as the detective moved about the room.

Cardona looked at the key upon the floor, near the door. He consulted the notes which had been given him. He knelt beside the body, and carefully examined the handle of the knife. Wrapping a handkerchief about it, he slowly withdrew the weapon from Harlew's body, and placed it upon a sheet of paper.

The knife was like a stiletto. It had a symmetry that was immediately apparent. The blade was rounded; it came to a long, tapering point. The handle was cylindrical.

Detective Cardona arose from beside the body.

"The window," he said, as he turned to Weston, "is inaccessible. No one could come up that wall without being seen. There are lights below, on the sidewalk. This key, however"—Cardona pointed to the floor—"gives us an answer to how the murderer entered. There is no evidence whatever that the door was locked."

"You mean before the murder?" asked Weston.

"Yes," returned Cardona. "Harlew was probably seated in that chair. The murderer entered. Harlew jumped up and saw him. As they grappled, the murderer stabbed him in the back.

"Before he left the room, the killer may have opened the window—or left it open. He took the key, closed the door behind him, and locked it from the outside. He shoved the key under the door, so it would look as though Harlew was trying to unlock the door when he died."

"Very good," agreed Weston. "You feel rather certain in that conclusion?"

"It looks logical, commissioner."

"Then"—Weston's tone was triumphant—"there is no doubt about this note. It is a hoax. A trick to deceive us."

Cardona looked up quickly. He saw the point of the

21

commissioner's argument. He nodded promptly, and voiced his agreement, although his words held a tinge of doubt.

"Yes," he said, "the murderer would have seen the note and destroyed it. But by planting the note, the murderer could put us off the track. There's only one way to figure it different."

"How is that?"

"By supposing that the murderer never got inside the room. If anybody can show me how that would be possible, I'd like to see it."

"Very good, Cardona," prompted Weston. "You can keep this note as evidence. It may incriminate the murderer when we apprehend him. But you are missing one point."

"What is that?"

"The murderer who wrote the note would scarcely have used the dead man's correct name."

Weston smiled triumphantly as he spoke. Cardona, however, came back with a prompt reply, referring to the notes as he made his remarks.

"There is a man named Schuyler Harlew," he declared, "who has an apartment about two miles from here. One of the men from the precinct checked up on him while I was on my way. Harlew has not been seen for three days. He answers this man's description."

"Ah! That is puzzling."

"I don't think so, commissioner," declared Cardona seriously. "It fits in perfectly. The murderer would figure that we would learn the dead man's identity. By putting Harlew's real name on the note, he makes it look like Harlew actually wrote it."

"Right," admitted Weston, throwing a quick glance toward Cranston, who had said nothing. "Very keen, Cardona. Very keen."

Weston caught Cranston's eye, and gave a slight nod as though to indicate that the millionaire had just heard a gem of deductive reasoning. Cardona rated highly in the commissioner's opinion. Now that the matter of the note to The Shadow had been settled as a hoax, all tension was relieved.

"We can go down to Harlew's place," suggested Cardona. "That's what I intended to do as soon as I had gotten a line on the murder situation. I've got a police car outside——"

"I shall go down there," interposed Weston. "Would you like to come?" He put the question to Cranston.

"Certainly," replied the millionaire.

Before departing, Weston took the police notations from Cardona and began to study the statements with which the detective had been working. Cardona watched him. The two stood alone, except for Cranston. Neither noted what the millionaire was doing.

While his tall form cast its mysterious silhouette across the dead body of Schuyler Harlew, the keen eyes of The Shadow were at work. It was amazing, the way they traveled from spot to spot.

A watch appeared in Cranston's hand. It slipped back into his pocket. With that action, The Shadow had checked the time upon the desk. A thin, knowing smile showed on the lips of Lamont Cranston. The Shadow had observed that Harlew's clock was fast.

Every detail of Harlew's antemortem statement was affixed in the keen brain of The Shadow. This master of deduction had observed points that had not occurred to either Cardona or Weston. They had read the note only word for word.

But to The Shadow, the one for whom that message was intended, the note was a revelation of Harlew's terror of an unknown foe. The Shadow knew that no murderer could have prepared such a document of human expression to lay upon that desk.

The doomed man's plea for aid rang true. The threat of death—the monster who wielded it—the hour of midnight —the suggestion of flight—the hesitancy about revealing the name—all were evidences of sincere statements.

Harlew's very suggestions that his thoughts were wild, that they would not settle until after the deadline of midnight, alone convinced The Shadow that the murdered man had inscribed the message to the one who he believed could meet and conquer the superfiend who had planned this death.

Why, then, if Harlew had written the note, had not the murderer taken it with him? Hasty flight on the murderer's part could not be the answer to his question. Cardona's theory included the deliberate locking of the door; the thrusting of the key beneath.

The Shadow saw the answer. It was one that Cardona had himself given, yet one which the star detective had rejected as impossible. The Shadow knew that Schuyler Harlew's murderer had never entered the room!

Strolling toward the window, The Shadow stood directly before the desk, at the very spot where Harlew had half risen from his chair. Staring through the crevice of the half-opened window, The Shadow, still wearing the thin smile of Lamont Cranston, saw an object at an angle across the street.

Cranston's limousine was parked beside it—a tall telephone pole that bore a thick grouping of wires upon its lofty cross bars. A pole of unusual height, the top of this pole was above the level of Harlew's window. The pole was barely visible against the evening sky.

"We are going, Cranston," remarked Commissioner Weston.

The burning of The Shadow's eyes had vanished as Cranston's tall figure turned from the window. That blaze reappeared for an instant as the same eyes focused themselves upon the stiletto that Cardona had placed upon the paper.

Outside the room of death, Commissioner Weston turned to look at the body as he had first viewed it. Cardona was beside him. The policeman was ready to close the door. Cranston, behind the group, was watching.

"Odd," remarked the commissioner, "the position of those hands. One over the other; fingers thrust out on the left; the right hand clenched, as though to fight the assailant."

"I noticed it," replied Cardona. "First thing when I came in. It's just one of those peculiar positions that you see with a lot of murdered bodies."

"Let's go along," suggested Weston. "And as for that note, Cardona"—he paused to tap the yellow paper which the detective held—"don't let it fool you. If this man whom we believe is Harlew had a name to give, why didn't he give it?"

"It looks fakey enough," agreed Cardona.

Lamont Cranston was still standing at the door as the commissioner and the detective started for the stairs. He, too, had noted the position of Schuyler Harlew's hands when he had entered the room. The eyes of The Shadow were keen. They were steadily fixed upon the dead hands when the policeman closed the door.

A whispered laugh, no more than a soft echo, sounded

from thin lips as Cranston walked along the hall to overtake the men who were descending the stairs. That was the laugh of The Shadow, given *sotto voce,* that none might hear. It was The Shadow's answer to questions which both Weston and Cardona had rejected as of minor consequence.

Schuyler Harlew had received his knife thrust at the desk. He had staggered away from the window; he had sprawled upon the floor. He had lost his opportunity—at the crucial instant—to inscribe the name of the man whose wrath he feared.

Dying, Harlew had tried to make amends for negligence. With the name of his enemy upon his lips, he had done his best to leave some trace of his final thought. Crossed wrists; three extended fingers; a loose fist. As The Shadow had viewed them from the door, they told a story.

Weston had not seen it. Cardona had not seen it. The Shadow, however, knew. From Schuyler Harlew's death-stilled hands, the master investigator had gained a vital clew to the identity of the monster who had doomed his minion to die!

With motionless lips, the lips of Lamont Cranston, The Shadow pronounced a single word that came as a startling aftermath to his solution of Schuyler Harlew's desperate effort to reveal a villain's name.

The left hand—three fingers spread with tips toward the door, denoted the letter "M." The right hand, with its loosely circled fist, gave the letter "O." The crossed wrists, placed with a final effort, stood for "X."

These were the letters which formed the name The Shadow uttered—a barely sibilant word that ended in a whispered hiss:

"Mox!"

CHAPTER IV

THE BROKEN TRAIL

It was well after ten o'clock when Commissioner Weston and Lamont Cranston joined Joe Cardona at the apartment where Schuyler Harlew had been murdered.

Again, Cardona took charge of the investigation, while Weston and Cranston watched. Harlew's apartment was plainly furnished. It was devoid of papers or any items that might have served as clews.

It was probable—Cardona set forth that fact—that the murderer had entered here to clean out house. Hunt high and low, the detective could find no shred of useful information.

Harlew had been a man who lived alone. He came and went as he chose. His occupation was unknown. His rent, however, was always paid well in advance. He had last been observed by people in the small apartment house three days before.

Cardona thumbed a Manhattan telephone directory. He shook it to see if it contained loose papers. He tossed the big book to the floor. It fell with opened cover near Weston's feet.

The commissioner paid no attention to the directory. He was watching Cardona pull out a table drawer. Cranston, however, stared toward the book. His sharp eyes spied a faint trace of penciled writing. For the first time this evening, Cranston offered a quiet suggestion to Joe Cardona.

"Look at the cover of the telephone book," he remarked.

Cardona wheeled, glanced at the speaker, then picked up the directory and laid it on the table. Under the glare of a lamp, the faint trace showed plainly. Cardona made out the initials B—U; the figures 2—6—8—0—4.

"Burset 2—6804," announced the acting inspector. "Say—that must be a number that Harlew called. It's a Manhattan number—around the Seventies, likely."

26

The detective picked up the telephone. Commissioner Weston, staring at the telephone book, noted that the number had evidently been erased, but not thoroughly. He wondered at Cranston's excellence of vision, then as he eyed Cardona, the commissioner made a quick protest.

"You're not calling that number——"

"No," returned Cardona. "I'm going to get headquarters. I'll have Markham locate it and phone me a report. After that, we can get down there."

Markham, a detective sergeant at headquarters, responded to Cardona's call. After giving him instructions, Cardona hung up and waited for a reply. It came in twelve minutes. Cardona gave prompt instructions; then turned to the others.

"The place is an old apartment building with a single telephone," he said. "Markham is going up there. We can meet him. The manager apparently lives in the building. East Seventy-ninth Street."

The trio rode in Cranston's limousine. When they reached their destination, Markham was awaiting them, with another detective. He announced that other men were watching the house in case a raid should be necessary.

"We'll see the owner," decided Cardona, pointing toward a window on the ground floor.

Weston nodded. Cardona had picked out the window because it bore a sign: Apartments To Let.

A quizzical, middle-aged man answered the door. He shrank back as Cardona exhibited a badge. He began to talk in a worried, pleading tone. Cardona motioned the others into the small room that served as a rental office, and began to talk.

"Your name is Mursled?" he questioned, following information received from Markham.

The man nodded, incapable of speech.

"Who's been getting calls here beside yourself?" Cardona pointed to the telephone as he spoke.

"The tenants," replied the middle-aged man, still using his wheedling voice. "They come down from upstairs. I let them use the telephone, if they do not ask too often."

"Who are the tenants?"

"The old lady on the second floor front; the two women who have the second floor back. The third floor front is empty. But the third-floor back apartment——"

"Who lives there?"

27

"The man you must be wanting. His name is Greerson—Peter Greerson. He has money, but not much. He always pays regular——"

"What is his occupation?"

"He says he is an inventor. I have seen him bring in big rolls of paper, with drawings on them."

"He's upstairs now?"

Mursled shook his head painfully. His face took on a wry expression.

"Mr. Greerson has gone out," he declared. "He has gone out to stay away, maybe. He stops in here—in this room —tonight. He tells me he may not come back. He says he expects to get money from somebody. He has drawings with him—and he says that if he does not come back, the things upstairs are no good unless he sends for them."

"Did he have a suitcase?"

"Two of them. Big ones. Why not? I do not stop him from going. He is paid in advance."

"Take a look upstairs, Markham," ordered Cardona. Then, as the detective sergeant left to obey instructions, Cardona again turned to the middle-aged man. "What time was this?"

"It was quarter past ten," said Mursled. "Mr. Greerson, he is in a great hurry when he comes in. I think he takes a taxicab outside. I am not sure."

"It's nearly half past eleven now," growled Cardona. "That's given him an hour to make a get-away."

Mursled, blinking through a pair of spectacles, showed interest at Cardona's remark. The proprietor of this converted apartment house was one of those individuals whose curiosity is more pressing than fear.

"What is it that you want Mr. Greerson for?" questioned Mursled.

"Murder!" retorted Cardona, swinging savagely toward the man whom he had quizzed.

"He has killed a man?" Mursled was aghast.

"A man has been killed," rephrased Cardona, staring narrowly at Mursled. "A man who knew this telephone number. A man named Schuyler Harlew."

"Harlew?" Mursled gasped the name eagerly. "I heard Mr. Greerson talk to him—one week ago—on this telephone. I heard him say the name. Harlew."

"What was the conversation about?"

"I don't remember, sir. I just remember the one name, Harlew. That was it. Harlew."

Markham came in while Cardona was still staring at the middle-aged apartment proprietor. The detective sergeant informed that he had entered the rear apartment on the third floor.

"Nothing much up there," announced Markham. "It looks as though the man has packed up and left."

"I'm going up," returned Cardona. "Take charge of this man, Markham."

Mursled sank into a chair. His voice was pleading as he insisted that he had done nothing. Cardona swung on his heel. Followed by Weston and Cranston, he strode up the stairs.

In Greerson's apartment, Cardona found matters much as Markham had described them. The place was illy furnished. It was untidy; but among the articles that had been left strewn about there seemed nothing of consequence.

A sheet of heavy drawing paper was thumb-tacked to a draftsman's easel. Odd piles of paper showed only rough plans of mechanical devices. A few tools, pieces of broken electrical apparatus: these were the only articles that remained.

"Looks like an inventor's hangout," observed Cardona. "This stuff may be faked, though. Maybe this fellow Greerson was just posing as an inventor."

After a short deliberation, the detective turned to Commissioner Weston. Tersely, he put forth his opinion.

"Commissioner," declared Cardona, with emphasis, "this is as far as we're going to get to-night. We know that Schuyler Harlew, the murdered man, must have made telephone calls to this house.

"The question is, whom did he call here? He may have wanted to talk to Mursled, the man downstairs. He may have wanted some other party, whom Mursled could reach. In either event, Mursled could throw it on to an imaginary person up in this apartment.

"But I watched Mursled when I quizzed him. He looks like what he claims to be—just the proprietor of a would-be apartment house, who lives in his own building. If there's anything phony in his story, I'll find it out soon enough.

"In the meantime, I'm going on the assumption that there is a Peter Greerson—a man who claimed to be an inventor—who lived in this apartment. He's the man we want."

"For the murder of Harlew," returned the commissioner.

"Yes," decided Cardona. "The trail is broken. But I'll pick it up, and at the end of it, I'll find the murderer. Peter Greerson is the man I'm after right now!"

"Sound theory, Cardona," commended Weston. "I must compliment you, Cardona, upon the effective way in which you have followed the trail this far. Continue the good work, until you locate Peter Greerson."

With Lamont Cranston, the police commissioner descended the stairs. On the way down, Weston added to the comments which he had made in Cardona's presence.

"Cardona is the best man at headquarters," he said, in a confidential tone. "He has a natural aptitude for rejecting the useless and keeping the useful. He gets to the point of crime. Sometimes he makes mistakes—he is intuitive, you know—but to-night, he has been at his best.

"It is obvious that Peter Greerson took to flight one hour before he arrived. The bird has flown the nest. Cardona will do his best to restore the broken trail. When Greerson is located, we shall have the murderer."

"Exactly," agreed Cranston.

There was a subtle note in the millionaire's remark. Weston did not catch it. He did not sense the sarcastic touch. He did not know that through the mighty brain which lay behind the masking countenance of Lamont Cranston was running a train of subtle thought.

The Shadow was thinking of the words in Schuyler Harlew's note: *"Death has been the lot of others. . . . Death will continue. . . . I have aided a monster in his schemes of death. . . . Midnight is the hour which the monster chooses. . . ."*

Why had Schuyler Harlew emphasized those points? The Shadow knew the answer. The enemy whom Harlew feared was a man far more powerful than the missing Peter Greerson.

Commissioner Weston and Joe Cardona had rejected the message to The Shadow. That note, however, had reached its desired destination. In the guise of Lamont Cranston, The Shadow had read every word of its scrawled lines.

He could plainly see the connection between Schuyler Harlew and Peter Greerson. The threat of death hung over others; Peter Greerson was doubtless one. The inventor had hurried away with packed bags and folded plans. He was on his way, unsuspecting, to meet the master plotter who planned his doom!

A watch showed in Lamont Cranston's hand as the tall millionaire stepped into his limousine. Its dial showed twenty minutes before the midnight hour. A bitter smile appeared upon the thin lips—a smile that seemed to show keen regret.

For The Shadow knew the penalty of this broken trail. It meant that Peter Greerson had passed beyond the zone of safety. Somewhere—his present location unknown—the missing inventor was reaching a rendezvous from which he would not return.

Greerson had not escaped the police. He had merely eluded the protection of The Shadow. It was too late to save him. But there would be others, perhaps, whose plight would prove equal if intervention did not come their way. It would be The Shadow's task to save them.

Mox!

The name rested on The Shadow's silent lips. There was the villain whom the Shadow must uncover. Murder dotted the past career of Mox. Even now, the fiend was about to commit murder unmolested.

The finding of Peter Greerson would uncover the murderer, but the murderer would not be Peter Greerson. This was The Shadow's finding. Rarely was the master forced to bide his time while murder was in the making. To-night, however, such was the case.

As the limousine pulled up at the Cobalt Club, Commissioner Weston alighted. Lamont Cranston paused before he followed. Within the restricting confines of the car, a soft, ominous laugh whispered forth.

It was the laugh of The Shadow; a laugh that foreboded a struggle between this powerful avenger and the fiend who called himself Mox. Peter Greerson would keep his appointment with death. The midnight hour was too close to be thwarted.

But Mox, the slayer of Schuyler Harlew, the murderer of victims to whose list Peter Greerson would be added tonight, would pay for his temerity. Wherever he might be, no matter how strong his citadel, The Shadow would seek him out.

At midnight, a final victim would be added to the roll that Mox was keeping. Before his fiendish will could again find its outlet, the hand of The Shadow would intervene.

The laugh of The Shadow died. Lamont Cranston, strid-

31

ing toward the entrance of the Cobalt Club, overtook Police Commissioner Ralph Weston.

Together, they entered, The Shadow and the official who did not believe that The Shadow existed!

CHAPTER V

THE STROKE OF TWELVE

The fading laugh of The Shadow!

That sinister sound had its echo many miles from Manhattan. It came in the form of a dying hiss as the locomotive of a heavy train stopped at the darkened platform of a station.

One man alighted from the train. He was carrying two suitcases and a roll of long cardboard underneath his arm. He looked upward at the station sign, barely visible from the lights of car windows. He saw the name "Darport."

The train puffed from the station. As its rear lights glided past, a heavy-set man stepped into the feeble glow and accosted the arrival who was on the platform.

"Mr. Greerson?"

"Yes."

"I have come to take you to Mox. The car is waiting."

Taking the bags, the heavy man led Greerson to a parked automobile. The inventor entered the rear of the car; the heavy man took the wheel. The car swung away from the darkened platform.

The town of Darport, as Peter Greerson viewed it from the window of the sedan, was a fair-sized community. The station was away from the center of the town. The course which the driver was taking did not pass through the business district. It was close enough, however, for Greerson to observe the lights, which were still shining as the midnight hour approached.

The car took a broad, tree-lined avenue. It turned into a side street. It swung up a driveway. Peering from the window, Greerson saw that they were in the shelter of a huge, ramshackle house. The driver alighted and opened the door. Greerson stepped forth. The driver led him to the house, where a side door opened and Greerson was greeted by a tall, bulky servant.

The inventor felt a slight shudder as the door closed behind him. There was something about the servant's manner—coupled with the man's ugly face—that made Greerson sense a danger. His fears ended as the servant spoke.

"You have your note?"

Greerson drew a folded slip of paper from his pocket. The servant read it. He uttered a hoarse call; another servant appeared, as ungainly a fellow as the first. He received the paper, and stalked away along a gloomy corridor. Greerson could hear his footsteps ascending a stairway.

Long minutes passed as the inventor waited with the first servant. Then came the trudge of footsteps. The messenger had returned. In solemn tones, he announced:

"Mox will see you."

The man picked up Greerson's bags The inventor carried the cardboard roll. With the servant leading, the two started through the hallway and up a pair of creaky stairs that made a long, winding course.

They passed through a corridor on the second floor. It terminated in a comfortable sitting room, where a fire was burning in the hearth. Greerson removed his hat and coat. He looked about the room, and observed a dog that was resting in the corner.

Greerson recognized the animal as a Dalmatian, the species used as a carriage dog. Of medium size, its white coat evenly studded with distinct spots of dark brown, the dog was unquestionably a thoroughbred. As Greerson eyed it, the dog growled and raised its long, pointed head. It made no further sign of enmity, however.

An open book upon a table, an ash tray from which smoke was rising; both were signs that the room had been but recently occupied. Greerson supposed that Mox, the man whom he had come to see, would soon return. Instead the servant arrived.

"Mox is ready," he said. "You have articles to show him—in these bags?"

Greerson nodded. The servant picked up the bags. He led the inventor back along the corridor and stopped. He placed his hand against a panel. It moved upward and showed a lighted entry; beyond it, another panel.

The servant motioned Greerson into the opening. The

33

two stood in the square space; the servant lowered the panel behind them. Then he pressed the panel ahead. It rose, and Greerson saw a small, oddly furnished room.

There, a man was seated behind a low desk. The chair that he occupied had a very short back—a peculiarity which marked the other chairs which the room possessed. There was a low bookcase by the wall. Beyond the seated man, in contrast to the small size of the room, was a huge open fireplace, all out of proportion to the apartment.

It was the man, however, who interested Greerson. It was impossible to tell his height while he was seated; his age, though, must be advanced, judging from his appearance. The man wore a heavy gray beard, and a shock of bushy gray hair adorned his head.

"Have a chair, Mr. Greerson," cackled the old fellow. "Sit here at the desk. We must talk."

The servant had retired. Greerson brought his bags over to the desk and took a chair. He looked closely at the old man across the desk. He had a distinct impression, at this close range, that the beard and hair were false.

"To begin with, Mr. Moxton," said Greerson, "I was somewhat doubtful about coming here."

"Do not say that," returned the old man, in his shrill tone. "Do not call me Mr. Moxton. I am known as Mox. Call me that. I am Mox, the great adapter."

Mox stared with sharp eyes as he spoke. He saw the look of apprehension which appeared upon Greerson's thin face. The inventor was a frail sort of a man, who showed the effects of an indoor life.

"Remain tranquil, my friend," asserted Mox, with an odd chortle. "I, like yourself, am one who prefers retirement and seclusion. Our mutual friend, Schuyler Harlew, told me that he informed you of the fact."

"Harlew did," announced Greerson pointedly. "He told me that you paid large sums for inventions."

"I do," returned Mox. "I have great wealth, my friend. I am always willing to deal fairly with those who can supply me with practical inventions. Through Harlew, as my discoverer of obscure inventors, I have been of great aid to men such as you."

"I have my plans," said Greerson guardedly, "and also my models. I have brought them with me, on the understanding that you will pay the price I ask."

"Name the price."

34

"One hundred thousand dollars," gulped Greerson. Then, as Mox gave no sign, he added: "It should be worth a million, easily."

Mox nodded solemnly.

"I shall pay your price," he cackled. "Let me see the plans and the models."

As he spoke, he opened a drawer in the desk and drew forth piles of bank notes. Greerson gulped again. He unrolled his sheets of plans and placed them upon the desk. He lifted the bags and opened them.

"This device," he began, as he brought out a completed model, "will increase dynamo efficiency——"

Mox waved his hand by way of interruption. He was studying the plans.

"I understand," he said, in his high voice. "I rely much upon Harlew's report. He told me that you had perfected your invention, but that you did not have the means to continue with it."

"Exactly," admitted Greerson. "The patenting would take a long time. I needed money; I need it now. It would be a mistake to lay these plans before representatives of a large corporation. When I met Harlew, he showed an interest——"

Again, Mox interrupted; this time with a chuckle.

"You are right, my friend," he said, "this invention is worth much money to the man who develops it. I shall be that man. It is worth more, however, than you ask."

Reaching to the desk, Mox bundled up fifteen piles of notes; he placed the others back in the desk drawer. He set the stack that he had kept directly in front of Greerson's eager eyes.

"One hundred and fifty thousand dollars," chortled Mox. "Ten thousand in each packet. That is what I shall pay you, my friend. Come; we shall take the money to my living room. Your plans and your models are mine; they can remain here."

Greerson turned toward the panel. He was in a fanciful daze. In a few short minutes, the transaction had been completed. He had sold his invention for a half more than he had asked. One hundred and fifty thousand dollars! It was the fortune for which Greerson had been striving!

At the panel, Greerson turned inquiringly. Mox was still seated at the desk. The old man pressed a button; the panel came up. He waved his hand for Greerson to step into the entry. Greerson obeyed, noting that Mox was about to

35

press a second button, evidently for the outer panel beyond the entry.

Mox cackled gleefully. From the entry, Greerson stared. He saw the old man, clutching the pile of money with his long left arm, his right hand upon the button. He saw a clock directly above Mox's head. The clock was whirring. Its chimes began to strike the hour of midnight.

Mox pressed the button. A wild cry came from Greerson's lips. The floor had dropped beneath him, splitting in the center. The inner panel was falling. As Greerson plunged downward, screaming, he made a hopeless clutch. It gained him nothing. His fingers slipped as they struck the smoothness of the dropped panel.

Wailing an instinctive scream, Peter Greerson went to the doom that Mox had prepared for him.

The old man did not hear the cry, nor did he hear the crash as Greerson's body shattered in a stone pit at the bottom of the deep, dark shaft. The dropped floor had risen shut. The panel was closed. All sound was drowned.

Peter Greerson's plans, his models, had been gained by Mox. The plotting fiend had stolen the fruits of the inventor's genius. Greerson, instead of Mox, had paid the price: with death.

While the slow chimes of the clock continued, Mox bundled the money back into the table drawer. He stalked to the panel and opened it by pressure. He stepped into the entry—no longer a danger spot—and raised the outer panel. The panels dropped as the clock completed the stroke of twelve. In the corridor, Mox cackled as he walked with stooped shoulders toward the living room where the Dalmatian reposed in the corner, and the fire burned merrily in the hearth.

A figure appeared at the entrance to the room. It was a servant whom Greerson had not seen; a curious, dwarfed sort of man who had evidently been hiding somewhere in the living room. Mox chuckled as he observed this short creature, whose form seemed all legs and arms.

"Another, master?" queried the dwarf, in a hoarse tone.

"Yes," trebled Mox. "Another. The last was yours, Sulu; this one was mine. We shall both have more."

The dwarf displayed fanglike teeth in an ugly, brown-faced grin. He stepped aside to let his master pass. With a short, bouncing stride, this spidery satellite followed his ruler into the living room.

The hour of twelve had struck. Mox, the murderer, had sent another victim to an unexpected death!

CHAPTER VI

THE SHADOW MOVES

A light shone in The Shadow's sanctum. It was a bluish glare, which clung to the top of a polished table, projected there by the incandescent above.

A pair of white hands rested on the table. From the third finger of the left hand shone a gem of ever-changing hue. This was a girasol, or fire opal, of rare size. It was the lone jewel which The Shadow wore, and its sparkling depths, with their intermittent flashes of light, betokened the mystery of The Shadow himself.

A stack of clippings appeared. Deft fingers separated them until only two remained. These were of varied dates; they came from different cities.

One told of the disappearance of an eccentric inventor, Joel Neswick, who lived in Philadelphia. The other mentioned another inventor, Curry Durland, who had left Cleveland for a journey East, and who had not returned.

Upon a white sheet of paper, The Shadow inscribed a single name of three letters: Mox. Beneath it, in separate columns, he wrote two other names, so the list read:

Mox

Schuyler Harlew   Peter Greerson.

The Shadow paused. He studied the clippings. He touched the more recent one first. It was the item from the Cleveland newspaper. Then, with deliberation, The Shadow added to his list. Its final context read:

Mox

Schuyler Harlew   Peter Greerson
                                         Curry Durland
                                         Joel Neswick

37

Thin lines appeared as The Shadow drew them from Harlew's name to those of the three inventors. Speculative though the list was, it asserted a definite truth.

Schuyler Harlew had contacted Peter Greerson, Harlew had admitted, in his statement, that he had led men to a monster who had designed their death. In his last living effort, Harlew had spelled the name of Mox.

Thus—as The Shadow reasoned—Peter Greerson had gone to visit Mox. The one feature that distinguished Greerson was the fact that he was an inventor. Thus, from a list of missing men, The Shadow had chosen others who were inventors also.

Perhaps Durland or Neswick did not belong upon the list; conversely, there were unquestionably others whose names did belong there, but whose disappearances had not been recorded. Joe Cardona would have been amazed had he seen The Shadow's list. It would have given him an inkling of the truth in this case.

Cardona was seeking Greerson as a murderer, not as a victim. It would not occur to the star detective to study the affairs of other inventors who might have disappeared. Cardona, with this list, might have begun an investigation of the past.

Therein lay another point that showed the detective's methods as puny when compared to the efforts of The Shadow. For The Shadow, as he viewed his list, was thinking of the future, not of the past.

Peter Greerson had followed the lure after Schuyler Harlew had died. The tapping forefinger of The Shadow's long right hand showed that this was the thought within the master brain.

Some other victim might soon be on his way to the lair which The Shadow knew existed—the unknown abode of the fiend whom Harlew had dreaded: Mox!

Upon a fresh piece of paper, The Shadow inscribed short statements, with a new pen from which flowed ink of vivid blue. These markings were like crystallized thoughts. They showed the working of The Shadow's mind.

As the ink dried, each written item faded. The fluid was a type that disappeared and left no trace.

Inventors.

The Shadow was thinking of men of Greerson's class, who might be here in New York. Any who would follow

Greerson were probably in the city, or would come here on their way.

Burke.

To look up such inventors would be the reporter's mission. Harlew had located such men; Burke, by effective work, might find one or more whom Harlew had filled with the impulse to visit Mox. His connection with the *Classic* would aid him in this.

Greerson.

The Shadow's hand paused as it placed the inventor's name upon paper. As the word faded, The Shadow added:

Departure.

Then, as a final thought:

Station.

Greerson, so the proprietor of the apartment house had said, had carried two large bags with him, and had taken a taxicab at a quarter past ten. The fact that Greerson had been in a hurry indicated that he must be intending to take a train.

Thus the time of his departure from either the Grand Central or the Pennsylvania Station would have depended upon a quick cab trip from the Seventies. Any train which Greerson might have taken would have gone out before eleven o'clock.

The Shadow's reasoning was apparent as his hand inscribed the names of the large terminals. But The Shadow did not overlook other possibilities; the railroads which left from New Jersey depots, accessible by tube or ferry from Manhattan. With these, as well as the large stations in New York, the departure could be set close to eleven o'clock.

Had The Shadow stopped with this, his tracing of Peter Greerson would have been ended. The Shadow, however, added another notation: one which was a recollection of a phrase in Schuyler Harlew's statement, found on the dead man's desk.

Midnight.

That lone word told its own story. Midnight! The hour which Harlew had feared; the hour at which Mox, the monster, dealt his strokes of death! A weird laugh crept through The Shadow's sanctum. Whatever Peter Greerson's destination may have been, the doomed man must have reached it amply before midnight!

The Shadow's hands disappeared. When they returned, they carried a folded map. They spread the chart upon the table. Then came schedules of train departures. His hands moving rapidly, but with no apparent effort, The Shadow began his consultation.

His long fingers produced white-headed pins, and thrust them into spots upon the map. When the time-tables were thrust aside, portions of the map within a fifty-mile radius of Manhattan were studded with markers that showed possible destinations where Greerson might have gone.

The process of elimination began. Studying certain pins, The Shadow removed them. Yet his quest had by no means been narrowed to a few points. Connecticut, New Jersey, Long Island, and points along the Hudson River showed indicative pins that might any one have been the spot The Shadow sought.

Roughly, the places which The Shadow had chosen formed an arc, with Manhattan as the center of the partial circle. Although a week or more would be required to visit all the possible towns by going in and out of New York by train, an automobile would make it easy to perform a circling tour.

Placing sheets of paper upon the map, The Shadow formed two itineraries. He sealed each in a separate envelope, and addressed one to Clifford Marsland, the other to Harry Vincent. Using the ink that would disappear when it encountered the air, The Shadow coded a message on a third sheet of paper. He folded the note and placed it, with the small envelopes, into a large envelope.

With indelible ink, The Shadow addressed the long envelope to Rutledge Mann, Badger Building, New York. Mann was a contact agent of The Shadow. He would receive this letter at his investment office. He would understand the code, reading it before it disappeared. As a result, Mann would communicate with Marsland and Vincent.

They were active agents. Each would take a different

route. In the towns which The Shadow had chosen, they would seek a man whose name resembled Mox.

The map showed large cities within close radius of New York. None of these were marked with pins. That was a sign of The Shadow's intuition. He knew that if Mox had sought a lair in an urban district, he would prefer New York to all other cities. Its massed population would offer much greater possibility for a hidden abode.

Since Peter Greerson had probably left New York by train, The Shadow, therefore, worked on the assumption that Mox had chosen the opposite type of district for his place of residence. The neighborhood of a small or fair-sized town would be the fiend's most likely choice.

The light clicked out. Darkness invaded The Shadow's sanctum. A chilling laugh resounded in the gloom. When taunting echoes had died away, the sanctum was empty. The Shadow had departed.

With his agents following the plans that he had directed, The Shadow could return to the places which Cardona had visited, and there try to take up the broken trail.

A grim course lay ahead. The Shadow was seeking to find the lair of Mox, before the murderer could strike again!

CHAPTER VII

TRAILS CONVERGE

Lamont Cranston was standing in the lobby of the Cobalt Club. A cigarette between his thin lips, the millionaire seemed lackadaisical. Actually, he was keenly alert. Behind this complacent exterior of languor lay the intuition of The Shadow.

This was the second night since Peter Greerson had disappeared. During the intervening period, the tall figure of Lamont Cranston had been seen but occasionally within the Cobalt Club. There was a reason; during both evenings, The Shadow had been conducting investigations of his own.

Garbed in obscuring garments of black, he had revisited the room where Schuyler Harlew had died, the apartment where the man had lived before, and the rooms which Peter Greerson had occupied on Seventy-ninth Street. Despite the thoroughness of the examinations, The Shadow had gained no clew to Mox, the man whom he sought.

Harlew—or some enemy of the dead man—had destroyed all traces. Greerson had left nothing by which he could be tracked. For once, The Shadow had struck a blind trail.

Meanwhile, however, his agents had not been idle. Performing the routines imposed upon them by their hidden chief, they had been sending in reports through Mann and Burbank. So far, nothing of value had been learned through their efforts.

Lamont Cranston, at his location in the lobby, could watch the clock as well as the telephone booths. The hands of the clock were nearing eleven. If this were to be a night for murder, the odds now lay with Mox. Yet Cranston never moved. When he affected the calm demeanor of the millionaire, The Shadow always played the part, no matter how crucial the time might be.

A ring sounded from the phone booth. Cranston stepped in that direction. His calm voice answered the telephone. His tones were recognized. Across the wire came the statement:

"Burbank speaking."

"Report."

"Report from Burke. Has just learned of another inventor. Joel Neswick. Phone Gotham 5—6424. Specialist in television apparatus."

"Report received."

Hanging up the receiver, Cranston called the number which Burbank had given him. It proved to be a small hotel, as evidenced by the clerk's voice.

"I should like to speak to Mr. Joel Neswick," announced Lamont Cranston.

"Sorry, sir," came the abrupt reply. "Mr. Neswick checked out at half past ten this evening."

"His forwarding address?" was the question in Cranston's tones.

"He left none," answered the clerk. "He did not say where he was going. He has probably gone out of town."

The eyes of The Shadow peered from the phone booth.

42

They flashed as they saw the clock, with its hands indicating eleven.

Burke's discovery of Neswick had been made too late. There was no doubt of where this inventor had gone. The very fact that he had left his hotel at half past ten was a duplication of Peter Greerson's action.

Neswick, like the inventor before him, had started along the one-way path that led to Mox. Another victim was placing himself within the monster's power.

At the stroke of twelve, Neswick, like Greerson, would die!

Two nights before, The Shadow had been unable to thwart the evil deed of Mox, the fiend. To-night, the situation was duplicated. One hour to go; then oblivion for the man who was entering the enemy's lair.

Investigation at the hotel which Neswick had left would give The Shadow no opportunity to save the doomed inventor's life. The Shadow had merely gained the satisfaction of knowing that his deductions were correct.

The telephone rang as Cranston was rising to leave the booth. The millionaire answered it. The eyes of The Shadow were burning orbs as his ears recognized the voice of Burbank.

"Report from Vincent," came the methodical words.

"Report!" whispered The Shadow.

"Vincent arrived in Darport, after leaving Solswood. Has learned of a man named Jarvis Moxton, living in an old house on the outskirts of Darport. Vincent awaits instructions."

"Orders to Vincent." The Shadow's voice showed triumph. "Meet night train at Darport station. Intercept Joel Neswick, unless he receives further instructions."

"Orders received," came Burbank's reply.

Lamont Cranston stepped from the telephone booth. He crossed the lobby of the Cobalt Club. He appeared upon the sidewalk outside. He stepped into his limousine.

"Garage, Stanley," he ordered his chauffeur. "I intend to drive my speedster home to-night."

Six minutes later, Lamont Cranston was seated at the wheel of a huge, expensive car that loomed with unusual bulk. The hood of the low-slung car was of great length. This automobile was built for speed.

Beside him, on the seat, the driver had a bag which he

43

had brought from the limousine. As the speedster rolled out into the street, a hand opened the bag and drew forth garments of black. A few moments later, the body of the driver was obscured beneath a blanketing cloak of black; his features were hidden by the broad brim of a slouch hat.

Lamont Cranston had become The Shadow!

The train which The Shadow now knew Neswick must have taken was due at Darport at eleven forty. It would require twenty minutes before the speedster could reach the open road; even this depended upon the fact that the garage was located at an ideal spot for quick leave-taking from Manhattan.

After that came nearly twenty miles of open road. With these odds, the chances of The Shadow's arrival before Neswick reached Darport were virtually nil. Harry Vincent was dependable, but in a desperate situation, no man could compare with The Shadow.

The clock on the speedster's dashboard showed twenty-seven minutes past eleven as the big car reached the spot The Shadow wanted—the clear road ahead. The motor roared as the accelerator was pressed. Like a jagannath, the huge machine showed its power.

The speedometer showed the speed at ninety miles an hour. Onward roared the car, its motor tuned to greater swiftness. As it veered left to pass an automobile going in the same direction, another car, coming from the fringe of a slight curve in the road, blocked the path head on.

Even with its present speed, the speedster seemed to take a jolting leap ahead as it clipped in between the two cars to avoid collision. The speedometer pointer passed the hundred mark as The Shadow performed this daring maneuver.

The big car swerved with the slight curve; the firm hands at the wheel held it to its course. With speed hovering between ninety and one hundred, The Shadow swept onward.

A shrill whistle sounded. The Shadow laughed tauntingly as the noise came from behind. State police were trying to stop the massive car. They had begun a chase. Even a swift motor cycle was no match for The Shadow's speed.

The big car dropped to seventy-five as it took a curve, then the higher speed was resumed. The speedster swept past three cars in a row. Clicking miles were matched by

44

furious minutes. The clock marked the time at twenty-two minutes before twelve.

Darport was but a few miles ahead, the train was due there in two minutes. As The Shadow swung the huge car to a stretch of road that paralleled the railway, a strident laugh came from his hidden lips.

The rear lights of the evening train were showing less than a quarter of a mile ahead! The train was running late by at least three minutes!

With this opportunity present, The Shadow did not hesitate. The speedometer pointer passed the hundred-mile mark. The speedster whirled past the moving train at double the locomotive's pace!

A curve one hundred yards ahead was revealed by the powerful searchlight mounted on the speedster. The road veered to the right; a railway crossing sign was in view.

Without a single glance to the rear, The Shadow applied the brakes. The speedster slackened for the sharp turn. With calm precision, The Shadow swung the wheel as the car reached the low speed of twenty miles an hour. A shrill whistle sounded from the right. The train was approaching.

Up went the front wheels on the grade crossing. From the right came the gleaming headlight of the locomotive. It was bearing down upon the speedster at a rate of fifty miles an hour. The automobile seemed doomed, as it struck the nearer track at the crossing. Then, as it was fairly on the cross-over, it shot forward as The Shadow gave it speed.

The car leaped from the locomotive's path. It twisted to the left, taking another sharp turn. The locomotive missed its rear by a scant two feet.

The train thundered by, the engineer staring with bulging eyes. He expected to see the fortunate driver bring his car to a stop; instead, the speedster increased its speed and traveled onward.

It burst ahead of the locomotive. Its tail lights disappeared behind a clump of trees, just as the engineer began to slacken speed for the Darport station.

With dim lights only, the speedster cut down a side road that brought it to the depot in advance of the train. Even those lights were extinguished before the swift car came to a stop. Silently, The Shadow dropped from the side of his machine.

The approaching glare of the locomotive showed a man

45

standing beside a parked sedan, awaiting the train's arrival. The same light revealed another, not far from where The Shadow's car was located. As the glare ended, The Shadow approached the second man, whom he had recognized as his agent, Harry Vincent.

Above the din and rattle of the stopping train, Harry heard The Shadow's whisper as it came from the sinister darkness. He nodded as he obeyed an order, turning toward the direction of The Shadow's speedster.

"Report," came a whisper.

"Moxton's car," replied Harry, in an undertone. "Meeting the train——"

Steps were opening. A man—evidently Neswick—was descending from a coach.

"Report received," whispered The Shadow, still lost in darkness. "Take speedster. Follow instructions."

Harry climbed into the huge car. He waited. Watching, he saw the man by the sedan approaching Neswick as the train began to chug from the station. Something fluttered in Harry's lap. He clutched a folded piece of paper in his hand.

The lights of the sedan came on. The car started from its parking place. As it swung out toward the street, Harry Vincent stared. The rear light had twinkled twice. Something had momentarily obscured its glow.

As the sedan disappeared, Harry opened the note and read the hasty coded words which The Shadow had inscribed.

Back to crossing. Take road on this side of railway. Thus avoid pursuing police. Unique Garage in New York.

Harry turned on the lights. He started the motor, and shot the big car to the road alongside the railway. He reached the crossing, but kept straight ahead. As he rolled down a side road amid trees, he heard the rattling chug of motor cycles.

The Shadow had far outdistanced the police. They would be on his trail, however, looking for the huge speedster in Darport or beyond. Harry's own car was near the Darport station. That did not matter. He knew The Shadow could find it if he needed it. Otherwise, Harry could return and get the coupé on the morrow.

As he drove along, however, Harry was wishing that he could have remained in Darport. Once he had located Jarvis Moxton's house, by cautious inquiry, he had been positive that it must be the place The Shadow sought.

The Shadow, however, had gone to face danger alone. Harry knew the reason for the blinking of the tail light on Moxton's sedan. The Shadow, riding on back of that vehicle, was going as extra passenger, to witness the interview that would take place between the owner of the old house and the visitor who had come by train from New York.

Harry Vincent knew nothing of the details. In his duty as an agent of The Shadow, he took orders and followed them. He wasted no time in idle speculation. Nevertheless, his common sense told him that The Shadow's errand to-night must be one that involved great danger.

In this surmise, Harry Vincent was correct. Jarvis Moxton, who called himself Mox, was a man who dealt in murder to gain his wealth.

The Shadow, like Joel Neswick, was going into the monster's lair, there to foil the death that had been set for the hour of midnight!

Trails had converged. The path of Joel Neswick, prospective victim, had been crossed by that of The Shadow, master of vengeance. Both would join within the weird house where Mox, the slayer, held his evil abode!

CHAPTER VIII

IN THE HOUSE

The sedan rolled up at the side of the old mansion. The driver alighted and opened the door for Neswick. Neither man saw the figure that dropped from the rear bumper of the car. The Shadow melted into darkness.

Neswick was visible as the door of the house was opened. The Shadow, peering from the night, saw the ugly-faced servant who had admitted him. He also caught a glimpse of Neswick's profile. The inventor was a man with sharp, determined features.

Beyond the space within the door, The Shadow saw the

47

gloomy hallway that led to the stairs. The fellow who had driven Neswick from the station returned to the sedan and drove it to a shed in back of the house. This spot evidently served as a garage.

The Shadow knew that quick action was necessary. He also realized that the man who had admitted Neswick could not be Mox. It still lacked nearly a dozen minutes before midnight. That was the time when the blow would fall.

Circling the house and shed, The Shadow spied lighted windows at the other end of the second story. Pressing his form flat against the side of the house, The Shadow began an upward course.

Like a creature of the dark, he gripped projecting portions of the stone wall and reached the level of the second-story window. The closed sash was curtained; it was also locked. Noiselessly, The Shadow pried the fastening open with a thin sliver of black steel that he wedged between the portions of the sash. He raised the lower half of the window a bare inch.

With gloved hands gripping the sill, The Shadow peered into the living room. He could see the flare of the fire in the hearth. He observed the Dalmatian serenely resting in a corner. The dog did not sense the intruder's presence.

Footsteps sounded in the hallway. Joel Neswick appeared, conducted by the second servant. The attendant informed the visitor that Mox would see him immediately. He walked out.

During the minute that passed after the servant had left the room, the sharp eyes of The Shadow studied the inventor more closely. Neswick bore the marks of genius. He seemed to be a meditative type of man, preoccupied with his own thoughts; at the same time he appeared capable of action at a critical moment. It was upon this that The Shadow based his plans.

Had Neswick appeared less capable, The Shadow would have entered to warn him. Instead, the watcher from the dark remained at his hidden post. He was ready to let this game continue until Mox, the murderer, had revealed his hand.

The servant returned to inform Neswick that Mox was ready to interview him. It was not until the two had left the room that The Shadow moved. Slowly, his black hands raised the sash. His keen eyes peered about the room. His tall, lithe form came over the sill.

48

The coach dog raised its head. A low growl came from its throat. The burning eyes of The Shadow shone toward the dog. The Dalmatian settled its head between its paws and blinked. The Shadow lowered the sash without noise.

Stealing to the door of the room, The Shadow peered along the hall. He saw the servant standing at a spot some distance from the room, with Neswick beside him. The hall was gloomy. It held opportunity for The Shadow.

Like a specter, the tall visitant eased toward the hallway. Momentarily motionless, his form was a blackened statue. Across the floor lay The Shadow's shadow; its silhouetted profile wavered with the flickering of the lighted fire.

While The Shadow prepared to advance along the hall, a silent action took place within the room. The door of a cupboard—in a corner which had not been visible from the window—opened. From it came the hunched creature with the spidery legs, the dwarf whom Mox had called Sulu.

The cupboard was the hiding place of this evil wretch. Through a tiny peek-hole, Sulu had seen The Shadow enter. Reaching the floor, Sulu glared with venom. His spidery arms raised from his baggy blouse.

Despite the noiselessness of Sulu's appearance, The Shadow sensed the creature's presence. As the dwarf's thin arms came up, The Shadow turned his head. His eyes, blazing over his right shoulder, glimpsed the evil monster.

The black cloak swished as The Shadow whirled; not toward the room, but out into the hall. Simultaneously, a long, thin knife blade whizzed through the air.

Aimed for The Shadow's back, it missed its mark by the scant fraction of a second. The Shadow, turning back toward the wall, was saved from death.

The point of the swift blade penetrated the flesh of The Shadow's left arm, just beneath the shoulder. A sharp stroke, but one which missed the bone, it pinned The Shadow to the wall.

The master fighter never faltered. The wound, though sudden, was no more than superficial. His right arm swung into action; an automatic blazed its reply to Sulu.

Chance saved the dwarf. The frame of the door intervened. The Shadow's bullet, directed with only a narrow margin, missed the dwarf by inches. Sulu made a dive for safety.

The second shot from The Shadow's gun clipped splinters from the woodwork, but, like the first, it could not get the hideous creature who was just outside its range.

Sulu had fled; The Shadow, still flat against the wall, turned his head along the hall. The servant was drawing a gun.

Neswick, looking vainly for the shots, and not observing The Shadow, happened to glance at the servant's face.

In an instant, the keen-minded inventor knew that danger lay not with the one who had fired, but with the servant. He saw the hideous, brutal features of the man. He sprang to wrest away the underling's gun.

The servant fired wildly, his bullet whizzed past The Shadow's head. The Shadow's finger was on the trigger of the automatic. It rested there. The Shadow could not fire, for Neswick had come between him and the servant.

A hand swung in the air. It held a revolver. The servant was swinging a blow for Neswick's head.

The Shadow fired. A scream echoed through the hall as his bullet caught the descending wrist. The barrel of the revolver glanced from Neswick's head. The servant, plunging to the floor with the inventor, scrambled wildly to pick up his dropped gun with his left hand.

The Shadow coolly used the interim. His automatic dipped into the folds of his cloak. With his free right hand, he gripped the handle of the knife which had pinned his left arm so mercilessly. He plucked the weapon from his flesh and threw it to the floor of the living room.

The servant had gained his gun. He raised it and fired with his unsteady left hand. The Shadow, his left arm at his side, was whirling as the shot went wide. His automatic came forth in his right. The evil servant sprawled as The Shadow's next shot found a vital spot in his body.

The roar of the automatic still persisted as The Shadow backed into the living room. His quick eyes turned in the direction which Sulu had taken. The dwarf had scampered to an adjoining room. The door was closed.

Blood, dripping from The Shadow's wounded arm, formed a crimson splotch upon the carpet. The Shadow did not heed the wound. His quick glance saw the Dalmatian moving in the corner. The dog seemed restless, but it did not advance.

There was no danger here; the new attack would come from below. Pounding footsteps on the stairs told that fact.

With swift stride, The Shadow advanced to meet the foe.

He reached the center of the hall as a servant thrust his head from the top of the stairs.

A revolver flashed in the foeman's hand. Before the arrival could fire at The Shadow's figure, he was met by the burst of the powerful automatic. The servant fired as he staggered. Half kneeling, he continued to shoot.

The Shadow had no alternative. His second bullet, directed with cool precision, found the man's evil heart.

With his right arm, The Shadow encircled Neswick's body. The inventor, though not short of stature, was light. The Shadow stooped as he carried the man across his back, like a sack. With his unwounded arm encircling Neswick's legs, The Shadow started for the stairs.

It was an amazing sight, this spectral, wounded fighter, carrying a half-stunned man to safety. Yet this deed was but part of The Shadow's task. As he stalked through the hall, he whirled, to see that no enemy had appeared from behind. He reached the head of the stairs just as new footsteps announced the arrival of more minions of Mox.

Two henchmen came in sight as The Shadow turned in their direction. One was the driver of the sedan, returned from the garage; the other was another servant who had evidently been below. There was no chance for The Shadow to evade their gaze, nor to use the fading tactics at which he was so successful. His one advantage lay in his apparent helplessness.

It was this factor that made his enemies pause to aim their guns as evil curses came from their snarling lips. They saw the automatic in The Shadow's hand, alongside Neswick's knees; they did not think that the fighter in black could use it.

That was their mistake. The muzzle of The Shadow's gun moved as of its own volition. Shooting almost from the hip, The Shadow blazed his challenge to these minions of Mox.

There was no vacillation in The Shadow's response. Burdened, wounded, he had but one course to safety. His first shot downed the nearer of Mox's men before the villain could fire his pointed gun. The second burst of the automatic sent the second plunging.

The first man, caught by a perfect shot, was dying. The second, dropped by more rapid aim, managed to fire as he staggered down the stairs, but his shots were high. Then his own plight made him forget The Shadow. Dropping his gun, he clutched at the banister and missed.

Screaming, he whirled headlong down the steps, until his body crashed against the wall at the bottom. The man lay still. The Shadow did not watch his fall. With a final twist, the black-clad victor made his last glance along the corridor. Seeing no one, The Shadow started down the stairs.

Blobs of dripping blood marked The Shadow's trail. Unfaltering, The Shadow kept on, as he carried Neswick to the safety that lay below. At the foot of the winding staircase, The Shadow paused beside the body of the last ruffian whom he had conquered. He let Neswick's form glide to the floor. The inventor, regaining consciousness, managed to rise and cross the hallway.

The Shadow watched him from the foot of the stairs. Then came the shouts of men outside. As The Shadow listened to this sound, he suddenly sensed another noise from above. Whirling toward the stairs, he spied a stooped-shouldered man who had come to view the havoc below.

Mox!

The Shadow knew instantly that this gray-haired figure with its beard must be the evil master of this house. A furious cackle came from the fiend's lips as Mox spied the outline of The Shadow.

Up came the right arm with its automatic. The Shadow aimed at this monster, who had appeared once he believed his minions had won the fray. A revolver glimmered in Mox's hand, but the fiend ducked for the shelter of the upstairs corridor as he saw The Shadow's automatic on its way.

Shots rang out; the first was from The Shadow's gun; the second from Mox's revolver. Results were nil. The Shadow, weakened by loss of blood, was an instant late in the swerving aim which Mox's dive required. Had the villain not sprung for safety, he would surely have been slain.

Mox's shot, made while in flight, went wide and high of The Shadow. The evil keeper of this lair had evidently recognized his enemy. He did not reappear while The Shadow remained in readiness.

Men were pounding at the door. Shouted commands were heard. The Shadow thus identified the arrivals. The State police who had been searching for the speedster had hurried hither at the sound of ringing gun fire.

With a sudden return of his swift activity, The Shadow swung from view. He did not take the stairs as the police burst through the door. Instead, he dropped to a sheltering place of blackness that formed an alcove underneath the stairway. This was the nearest spot that enabled him to make a quick disappearance. Even Neswick, bewildered in the hallway, did not witness The Shadow's remarkable departure.

There was strategy in The Shadow's action. At the very instant when the police burst into the lower hall, Mox appeared at the head of the stairs. The fiend believed The Shadow trapped between two fires. Instead, he was startled to find himself face to face with two policemen who were dashing toward the steps.

Mox fired. His second shot clipped a State trooper's arm. The officer staggered. His companion returned the fire; with two others at his heels, he dashed up the stairs.

Quick, hasty shots resounded; then Mox, seeing three men moving to the attack, hastened down the corridor.

When the police arrived at the head of the stairs, there was no sign of the gray haired enemy. Mox, like The Shadow, had disappeared. Two officers began a search of the second floor. The third returned to join his wounded companion below.

Neswick had started to the wounded man's aid. Neither he nor the crippled policeman saw the phenomenon which occurred in the center of the hallway.

From his hiding place beneath the stairs, The Shadow moved forth like a ghost of the night.

A tall, gliding apparition, he gained the outer door. His tall form swayed as it reached the coolness of the night air. There, it seemed to regain its strength as it vanished in the darkness.

When next that form appeared, it was beside Harry Vincent's parked coupé, near the railroad station.

Merging with the darkness inside the car, The Shadow rested behind the wheel. His right hand found a roll of bandage in a side pocket. Harry Vincent, engaged on missions which promised serious results, never neglected to carry such equipment.

The bandage formed a snakelike strip of white amid a mass of blackness as The Shadow bound his wounded arm. The task completed, the dark sleeve of the cloak dropped to obscure the bandage. A single hand—The Shadow's right—gripped the wheel as the coupé pulled away.

A brisk reviving breeze reached The Shadow as he drove

53

away from Darport. His work was ended for this night. His wound, though painful and extremely weakening, would be forgotten within the next few days.

Sulu, the hideous dwarf, had served Mox well to-night; yet the spidery servant had failed to accomplish the real task given him. He had merely made The Shadow's fight more difficult.

He had not thwarted The Shadow's saving of Joel Neswick. He had not prevented The Shadow from eliminating Mox's henchmen. He had only managed to save his own hide, and to stop The Shadow from reaching Mox himself.

The Shadow, even then, would not have given up his quest but for the arrival of the State police. That episode had also played its part in the escape of Mox. The Shadow, however, had turned it to advantage. With Neswick rescued, he had played a quick game that had placed Mox face to face with the law.

Neswick's story would be believed. Mox would be sought. His lair would be of no more use to him. Such were the developments that The Shadow had brought.

Oddly, his quick trip to Darport, which had brought the police pursuit of the speedster, had played a definite part in the culmination of to-night's episode.

The Shadow had thwarted death at midnight. That was the great achievement. A sardonic laugh—tinged with a trace of weariness—emerged from the interior of Harry Vincent's coupé.

The murderous career of Mox had been suspended. From now on, the villain would have but one main purpose: to destroy The Shadow. That was the thought that had brought The Shadow's laugh.

The Shadow knew that a new struggle was commencing. His wits against those of a murderous supermind of crime. The law had intervened, but it would merely set the stage for the final drama.

The climax would be the next meeting between The Shadow and the fiend called Mox!

CHAPTER IX

CARDONA TAKES A TRIP

"What do you think of it, Cardona?"

Police Commissioner Ralph Weston was the propounder of the question. He had summoned the star detective to his office on the second morning after the affray which had occurred in Darport. He was pointing out the latest news reports of the amazing incidents in the house of Mox.

"Burke may be right," returned Cardona thoughtfully.

"Who is Burke?" inquired the commissioner.

"The *Classic* reporter," was Cardona's response. "He's written what I've been thinking. His link-up of missing inventors seems to hit the nail on the head."

"Then you see a tie-up with the Harlew murder?"

"I do. Commissioner, I've been reading that note we found on Harlew's desk. I think maybe the murderer left it there because he didn't see anything in it that would point us to the source of crime."

"But the reference to The Shadow! Preposterous!"

"The letter was simply addressed to The Shadow. Harlew may have been—well"—Cardona's tone was reluctant—"maybe he was goofy. I've been reading this fellow Neswick's story. He left New York at just about the same time of night that Greerson started out. They tried to get Neswick in this fellow Moxton's house. Maybe they did get Greerson."

"The newspaper reports," commented Weston, in a wise tone, "are somewhat garbled. I have discovered the reason."

"Do you mean the guy that's handling the case?" queried Cardona. "Junius Tharbel—the county detective that thinks he's a big shot?"

"Yes," replied Weston. "Tharbel is a big man—in a small way. As county detective, located in Darport, he has gained a remarkable record over a period of twenty years. He has made a name for himself, Cardona."

"As a sportsman," returned the detective.

"Yes, that's true," laughed the commissioner. "He likes fishing and hunting, and is quite a golfer, I understand. Well, Cardona, you can thank Tharbel for one thing. Your work as an acting inspector has ended. You will be relieved."

"On account of Tharbel?" Cardona could not repress the indignation in his question.

"Only indirectly," smiled Weston. "I have arranged with Tharbel to send a special representative of the New York police to Darport. You are the detective whom I have chosen for the job."

"That's different, commissioner." Cardona was somewhat sheepish after his outburst. "It suits me great. If there's any tie-up between this attempt on Neswick's life, and the disappearance of Greerson—as well as Harlew's death—you can count on me to uncover it."

When the noon express stopped at Darport, Detective Joe Cardona alighted to find a solemn, hatchet-faced man awaiting him. He recognized Junius Tharbel, the county detective who had gained so high a reputation in his section.

Tharbel, rather tall and something of a scarecrow in the old suit that he wore, extended a brief greeting to the New York sleuth.

He led Cardona to an old coupé. The car rattled along the rough streets of Darport, and pulled up in front of a dilapidated building where Tharbel's offices were located. The rear of the county jail was visible from the second-story room where Tharbel conducted Cardona.

"Where are the reporters?" queried Cardona.

"Somewhere around town," returned Tharbel tersely. "Playing some of these contraptions, I reckon."

He indicated a row of broken slot machines along the wall of his office.

"Picked these up on a raid," he explained. "There's new ones in; I'll grab them some day next week."

Joe Cardona repressed a grin. A county detective who bothered himself about nickel machines was small fry, in his opinion. But the response to Cardona's next query caused the New York detective to form a reluctant admiration for Tharbel's ability.

"I can't figure why the reporters aren't around," remarked Cardona. "They're usually hot on a job like this."

"They know me," answered Tharbel. "That's why they're

not here. The more they pester me, the less they get. I let them hang around until they're sick of it. One of them saw these machines. That gave him an idea of a way to spend his time. The others went along with him."

"The city editors will be wondering about the heavy expense accounts," commented Cardona, with a grin.

"Sit down," suggested Tharbel, as he took a chair behind a broken-down desk, and removed a stack of papers from a drawer. Cardona accepted the invitation.

"Here's what I've got," continued Tharbel. "The reporters are all mixed up about it. This is our confidential information."

Cardona nodded.

"State police," began Tharbel, in a matter-of-fact tone, "raided the home of a man called Jarvis Moxton, two nights ago, shortly after midnight. They heard shots. That's why they went into the place.

"When they entered, they were shot at from the head of the stairs by a man who answers the description of Moxton. An old fellow, with gray hair and beard. He wounded one of the State policemen. He got away.

"The police found the bodies of four dead men, all of whom have been identified as servants of Moxton. Besides, they discovered a man named Joel Neswick, whom they brought to me. I am holding him as a material witness."

"The inventor," remarked Cardona.

"Yes," declared Tharbel. "He was obviously intended to be the victim. Someone—evidently an enemy of Moxton—intervened to save him."

"The details?"

"I can give them. Joel Neswick came to see Jarvis Moxton to sell him an invention. He was suspicious of the house after he entered it. He was taken to Moxton's living room. Then he was conducted back through the hall.

"That, according to Neswick, was when the trouble began. There were shots from the living room. The servant who was with Neswick pulled a gun. Neswick struggled with him. He got a knock-out blow on the head.

"He remembers someone helping him. He was carried to the stairs and all the way along; this rescuer fired at the other servants. Neswick was dropped at the foot of the stairs. He was still bewildered when the police entered."

"And the man who helped him?"

"He was gone."

"Hm-m-m," commented Cardona. "Do you think Neswick's story is on the level?"

"Yes," snapped Tharbel, in a positive tone, "and I'll tell you why. First of all, everybody in the house belonged to Moxton. Second, Moxton battled the police. Third, Neswick had a chance to get away; instead, he helped the wounded State policeman who was lying alone. Fourth"—Tharbel's words were terse—"Neswick has stuck to his story about another person being there. It's the right story, too."

"But if this other man was not seen by the police——"

"Old Moxton's servants," interposed Tharbel, "were shot by bullets fired from a .45-caliber automatic. Neswick had no chance to hide a gun. He was unarmed. Moxton had a revolver, not an automatic."

"He might have used the automatic first."

"Yes. But I am sorry to say, I doubt it."

"Why?" questioned Cardona, in a puzzled tone.

"Because," declared Tharbel, "we want Moxton for the attempted murder of Joel Neswick. If my theory is right, we will want him for the murder of other persons. If we had proof that Moxton had killed the servants—which I am sure he did not—we would have a more immediate charge against him."

"But the man who did kill them——"

"Fought in self-defense, by Neswick's statement. He was there to prevent murder, and he succeeded."

Cardona was thoughtful. He was forced to admit to himself that Junius Tharbel was a detective of real ability. He was getting details that the local sleuth had kept from the reporters. More startling information, however, was immediately forthcoming.

"Murder," asserted Tharbel. "That's the charge I want to bring against Jarvis Moxton. That's why I have accepted your cooperation. You can supply the murder charge."

"You mean——"

"I meant that Joel Neswick has told us who sent him here. He came at the suggestion of a man named Schuyler Harlew."

"Who was murdered in New York!"

"Yes. But Neswick didn't know it. He was working on the final details of the invention he brought to Moxton. He had not read the newspapers for several days."

"That might be a stall."

"Not a bit of it. Why would Neswick mention Harlew's name, if Harlew wasn't in it? Would a man go out of his way to claim that he had not read the newspapers for a week? Listen, Cardona: I base my theories on my judgment of human nature. A crook will show himself, every time. If he tells a good story, it's a glib one. I'll let you talk with Neswick. You'll agree that I'm right."

"If we can get the man who murdered Harlew," declared Cardona, "we'll get the man——"

"Who murdered Greerson," interrupted Tharbel shrewdly.

Cardona found himself nodding in agreement. The county detective had taken the very thought that he had been about to express.

"The State police are guarding the old house," continued Tharbel. "They have found some very interesting indications, which the newspapers have missed. We can go over there shortly. In the meantime, I may add that the police captured a witness who has not yet made his statement."

"A witness? In the house? Did you hold him?"

"Yes. A Dalmatian."

"Doesn't he speak English? An interpreter would do the trick——"

Tharbel chuckled by way of interruption.

"The Dalmatian is a dog," he explained. "A carriage dog; the kind that used to run under coaches. White, with brown spots——"

"I've seen them on Fifth Avenue," nodded Cardona, "but that was a good many years ago. Say—if the breed is rare, you might be able to trace Moxton through the dog."

"Hardly," decided Tharbel. "No, the dog will be more useful later on—when we have found Moxton."

"You mean that the dog will know him?"

"Exactly. The dog, very fortunately, refuses to make friends. When I learned that fact, I had him placed in the jail. The men in charge of him have strict instructions not to coax him. No one—not even myself—has approached him. The dog wants his master. When he sees him——"

Tharbel did not complete the inference. Cardona again admired the county detective's shrewdness. A dog would know its master. Moxton's dog would probably be no exception.

"Not only Moxton's house," declared Tharbel, "but the man's own actions indicate his crookedness. He came here some months ago and purchased the old house for cash. It

59

underwent repairs. Moxton, when he lived there, posed as a semi-invalid. He was seen, nearly every day, by persons in the neighborhood, when he took feeble walks about his premises.

"But when he faced the State police, he showed every sign of agility. His disappearance is further proof that he could move with speed. He must have made his way out one of the many downstairs doors. There were two flights of steps in the house. He could have taken the ones opposite those which the police used to come up."

With this statement, Tharbel arose and picked up his hat. He motioned Cardona to come along.

"Can't show you the dog," said Tharbel abruptly, as the two men went down the street. "Nobody sees that Dalmatian. Not until we've got Moxton—nobody except the men who are looking out for him. But I'll take you to the house."

As they climbed into the coupé, Cardona put a sudden question. It was something that he had meant to ask, but had forgotten in the discussion of other matters.

"You say that all of Moxton's servants died?" he asked. "All lost out when they were fighting to get this inventor, Neswick?"

"All that we could find," returned Tharbel.

"And yet Neswick could give you no description of the man who rescued him?"

"Only a vague description," answered Tharbel, as he guided the coupé to the avenue which led to Moxton's house. "So vague, in fact, that it only shows that Neswick must have been knocked pretty hard when Moxton's servant hit him with the gun."

"What was the description?" persisted Cardona.

"Well," recalled Tharbel, "all that Neswick could see was flashes of an automatic. He felt himself lifted up, but everything was black while he was being carried downstairs. When Moxton opened fire from the top, he saw more flashes from the bottom. Then he imagined that he saw a lot of darkness move and spread like it was human. A black ghost—that's all that Neswick could describe."

Tharbel was staring along the road as he spoke. He was turning the car to bring it alongside of Moxton's house. Hence, the famous county detective did not see the gasping look that appeared upon Joe Cardona's face.

Yet in his remembrance of Neswick's blurred description, Junius Tharbel had given Joe Cardona final assurance that Neswick's story was a true one. The mention of a black ghost—a phantom shape that vanished before bewildered eyes—was all that Cardona needed.

The defeat of four armed henchmen by one lone fighter was explained to Joe Cardona's satisfaction. The sac detective had gained a positive hunch of his own. His lips silently framed the name of the being whom he was sure had won that fray:

"The Shadow!"

CHAPTER X

THE SECRET ROOMS

Junius Tharbel offered Joe Cardona a piece of chewing gum as the two detectives entered the old Moxton house. Cardona refused, with thanks. Tharbel calmly chewed the gum himself. The steady, even motion of his jaw seemed to add to the hatchet-faced man's complacency.

A State policeman greeted the visitors. He started to draw Tharbel aside to speak in confidence. The county detective restrained him with a gesture.

"This is Detective Cardona," he said by way of introduction. "He's from New York. Whatever you have to tell me, he can hear."

"It's about that prowler we saw last night," explained the policeman. "I thought we'd better have an extra man on duty in case the bozo comes around again."

"What prowler?" questioned Cardona, turning to Tharbel.

"I forgot to tell you about that," returned the county detective, in an annoyed tone. "I don't regard it as important, anyway. We've got to expect prowlers. Morbid-minded people like to come around a place like this."

"The guy was funny-looking enough," volunteered the State policeman. "I heard him near the house; I flashed a glim on him. He was going toward the old shed out back. When he saw the light, he went hopping away. He was all legs, that guy, with a midget body."

"I don't think you'll see him again," decided Tharbel. "Don't worry about an extra man."

"You can't be too sure about it," remarked Cardona.

"I'm handling this case," announced Tharbel abruptly. "You may be right about prowlers in New York. Out here, they're different."

He paused and looked about the hall. He pointed to a spot just within a door.

"This is where Neswick gave his note to the servant," explained the county detective.

"What note?" inquired Cardona.

"The one that Harlew gave him," returned Tharbel. "It was sort of an introduction card to Moxton. It was just signed 'Mox.' I told you about it at the office."

"No, you didn't," declared Cardona testily.

Tharbel was on the verge of an angry utterance. He restrained himself. Cardona broke the tension with a new query.

"What became of the note?" he asked.

"One of the servants took it upstairs," replied Tharbel, in a surly tone. "He must have left it up there, with Moxton. Neswick says he came back and ushered him upstairs. That's what I'm going to show you—the whole lay-out, and all that happened, as Neswick remembers it."

"All right," agreed Cardona.

In a matter-of-fact fashion, Junius Tharbel began the tour of inspection. The State policeman followed as the rural detective led his New York colleague through the old house.

"Neswick was brought upstairs," declared Tharbel, as the pair ascended the steps. "He was taken to this room"—the speaker paused until they reached the living room at the end of the corridor—"and he waited here a short while. He saw the dog lying in that corner. It growled at him.

"Then he was brought back to the center of this corridor. That's when the first shots came—from the living room. There seemed to be a fray beginning there. Neswick grabbed the servant here. The fellow clouted him with a gun. Then the servant got his—from the living room."

Tharbel indicated the spot where the body of the servant had been found. He led Cardona slowly toward the stairs.

"Neswick was carried," he described, "and the man who rescued him was firing. One of Moxton's servants was dropped here, another on the stairs. One rolled clear to the bottom. That was the last one."

"Four in all?"

"Yes. Four. But there may have been another—in addition to Moxton himself."

"Why?"

"The firing, Neswick says, came from the living room. There's a little room off it. One man may have gone in there and come out later. There must have been two people to start the shooting match in the living room."

"Where was Moxton?"

"I'll show you." Tharbel's eyes gleamed wisely. "This is one of the tips that Neswick gave us. While he was here"—Tharbel turned to point out the center of the corridor—"it looked as though the servant was going to take him to some hidden place. See these panels along the wall? Well, we tried them, and this is what we found."

Tharbel worked at one of the panels. It slid open. The county detective used a flashlight to show a long, narrow room, which resembled a corridor. The room was entirely empty. It was about five feet in width and twelve in depth.

"A hide-out," observed Cardona.

"Probably," agreed Tharbel, "and here is its mate."

Letting the panel drop shut, he led Cardona farther along the corridor, past a second panel to a third. He opened this one. His light showed another long room identical with the first.

"Two secret rooms," remarked Cardona.

"Yes," said Tharbel, "with a wall between."

"Do they connect?"

"No. We have examined each one thoroughly. The intervening wall is solid. It is very thick—close to six feet. It is probably the center section of the house—a sort of backbone on which the building depends."

"These rooms would account for Moxton's get-away."

"For a temporary hiding place, at least. Probably Neswick was to be thrust into one of these. Mox—or Moxton—whichever you choose to call him—may have been waiting to kill Neswick: Shots in one of these muffled rooms would not have been heard outside."

Junius Tharbel let the panel fall. He and Cardona went downstairs. The county detective remarked that the entire house had been ransacked. A third floor attic had revealed nothing. The cellar, outside of a few oddly shaped compartments, had shown no signs of hiding places.

A coolness had arisen between Cardona and Tharbel. Routine completed, each began to remember remarks which the other had made. The two went out to Tharbel's car, and rode back to the office building near the county jail.

Reporters were awaiting them. Joe Cardona was greeted by Clyde Burke. This was the making of a story; the arrival of the ace detective from Manhattan. The reporters— Burke in particular—wanted to know the reason. Joe Cardona referred them to Tharbel.

It was obvious that Tharbel gave the newsmen what he chose. Cardona noted that they gathered around the desk with a respectful attitude. The hatchet-faced county detective thought a while before he made his statement.

"Detective Cardona," he stated, "has come here because Joel Neswick testified that there is a connection between Jarvis Moxton and Schuyler Harlew, whose death Detective Cardona is investigating in New York."

Questions came from two reporters. Tharbel waved his arms to show that his statement had been made. He pulled a fresh piece of chewing gum from his pocket and picked the wrapper from it.

"Come along, gang," suggested Clyde Burke. "I told you to keep quiet and let Tharbel talk. You didn't; that's all you'll get."

As the reporters thumped down the steps, Tharbel made a sagacious comment to Cardona.

"Never let reporters ask questions," was his advice. "I give them statements; nothing more. Most of the questions that reporters put are leads that they twist around to suit themselves. Let them jump around with their crack-brained theories and build up the stories that their newspapers want. It's a help more than a hindrance, as I see it.

"They don't try much funny stuff with me, though. If they do, I let them down later on, when the case begins to clear. That's my rule: no questions answered. Statements, when I care to make them. It makes them behave, so they will get their statements."

"You didn't tell them much just now."

"I was going to tell them more. They spoiled it. That fellow Burke used his head. He cleared the crowd out when

64

he knew I was through talking. He knows when my statement is ended. A new stick of chewing gum; that's all."

Minutes of silence passed. Cardona felt mingled resentment and admiration. He was forced to admit that this hatchet-faced county detective was a capable individual; at the same time, he did not like the man's self-satisfaction.

Joe decided that Tharbel made it a practice to tell what he thought necessary, and keep the rest to himself.

That was not a bad idea. Cardona planned to follow the system himself. He felt sure that he had already learned one point which Tharbel did not know; namely, that the mysterious phantom known as The Shadow had battled the minions of Mox.

Whenever The Shadow appeared as an avenger of crime, remarkable consequences followed. Cardona knew that such had occurred before; he was positive that something of the sort was in the offing at present.

This case was the outgrowth of a dead man's message to The Shadow. Somehow, The Shadow might have learned the contents of the note. The Shadow, certainly, had reached Mox, the master of Schuyler Harlew, before any others had discovered the murderous old man.

Joe Cardona regarded The Shadow as an entity. He had many proofs of the power of the mysterious avenger. The Shadow's ways were The Shadow's own. When The Shadow took the trail to uncover crime, those who followed would invariably gain through The Shadow's findings. So Cardona resolved to say nothing of his hunch.

"I should like to talk to Neswick," said Cardona to Tharbel.

"You'll find him over at the Darport Inn," responded the county detective. "He's staying there as a guest; one of my men is with him. Start over if you want. I'll call Scudder—my assistant—and tell him that it's all right for you to talk with Neswick."

Cardona sauntered from the office. He reached the inn and inquired for Neswick. He was sent up to a large, comfortable room, where he found the inventor sprawled in a lounging chair. Scudder, the assistant detective, was with him.

Cardona introduced himself. Scudder had received the call from Tharbel. Neswick shook hands with the New York detective.

At Cardona's request, he repeated the story which

Cardona had learned from Tharbel. Joe came down to details which interested him specifically. He asked Neswick just what he knew about Schuyler Harlew.

"The man came to see me at my hotel," declared Neswick. "I liked Harlew. He seemed sincere when he told me that he had a purchaser for the television plans which I had developed. Harlew stated simply that he traveled for Jarvis Moxton; that the old man was interested in the purchase of inventions.

"One day, Harlew came and arranged for me to visit Moxton. That was about two weeks ago. At that time, Harlew gave me a note—simply a scrawled introduction signed 'Mox.' I was to give it to the servant when I arrived at Moxton's home.

"I was busy with my plans after that. I failed to read the newspapers that told of Harlew's death. I came to Darport; you know the rest. I am very sorry, indeed, that I cannot give you any worthwhile information that pertains to Schuyler Harlew."

Cardona nodded. He found himself agreeing with Junius Tharbel that Joel Neswick was a man who had told a straightforward story.

It was late in the afternoon when Cardona left the witness and went down to the hotel lobby. There he met Clyde Burke.

"How about dinner?" questioned the reporter.

"All right," agreed Cardona. "But I'm saying nothing, Burke. This is Junius Tharbel's precinct."

As reporter and detective dined, Burke brought up the subject of Tharbel. Like Cardona, the reporter regarded the county detective with antagonism as well as approval. He delved into Tharbel's odd methods.

"The hunting season is on," said Burke, with a smile.

"Tharbel's a hunter, isn't he?" queried Cardona.

"Best shot in the county," laughed Burke. "If he decides to go out after game, he'll let this case slide along. You wait and see."

"Great stunt for a county detective," snorted Cardona.

"They think a lot of Tharbel out here," reminded Burke. "He gets results, Joe. That's what counts."

"I guess so. Well, I'll drop over and say good-by to his nibs. I'm going back to New York."

"Tharbel will be at his home, Joe. I'll take you around there in my car."

66

When Cardona knocked at the front door of Tharbel's unpretentious home, the county detective, himself, was the one who answered the door. Cardona stated that he was going back to New York, that he might communicate with Tharbel later.

Joe extended his hand. Tharbel received it and said good-by. He closed the door as soon as Cardona had turned away.

In the car with Burke, Cardona grunted. He was glad that he was through with Tharbel for the time. Burke laughed as he backed the car to turn around in the street.

"You don't know Tharbel, Joe," he said. "That fellow just sits back and lets things break. He seems to know when events are going to turn his way. He always figures that someone is going to slip him some needed information.

"Talk about your New York stool pigeons—they're nothing. Tharbel always seems to be getting anonymous letters and what-not——"

"Any on this case?"

"None as yet—so far as I can see."

The glare of Burke's headlights had swung across Junius Tharbel's lawn. Cardona heard a gasp come from the reporter. The detective stared ahead. On the fringe of illumination, he caught a momentary glimpse of what appeared to be a huge, living spider, leaping away from the glare.

"What was that?" he queried.

"I don't know," responded Burke, as he swung the car to the street. "Some person, maybe, cutting across lots in back of Tharbel's. It may have been an animal. The lights make shapes appear odd."

Burke was driving toward the station. There were only a few minutes in which to make Cardona's train. The reporter had suddenly assumed his secret role, as agent of The Shadow. He made no further comment.

Cardona, too, was silent. He was thinking of what the State policeman had said.

A spidery creature—all arms and legs—had been seen near the house of Mox. Junius Tharbel had decided that an additional watcher was unnecessary. Now, Joe Cardona had seen a distorted creature near the home of Junius Tharbel.

The star detective pondered over these matters as he rode toward New York in the train. He also thought of the secret rooms in the old house. He wondered what their purpose might be—if other than a hide-out.

Most of all, Joe was thinking of Tharbel. He decided that Burke was right. The county detective was playing a cagy game.

Joe Cardona had a hunch. He felt that he would soon encounter Junius Tharbel again, and that future meetings would involve a battle of wits between himself and the smart county detective.

CHAPTER XI

WEIRD VISITORS

As soon as he had reached the Darport Inn, Clyde Burke made a telephone call. It was not to the *Classic* office. The call was made to Burbank. Clyde reported his observation of a distorted, long-limbed creature in the neighborhood of Tharbel's home.

The call put Burke off duty. Nevertheless, The Shadow's agent could not shake off the thoughts that the sight of the monstrosity had given him. Clyde Burke, like Joe Cardona, was puzzled by events which had occurred in Darport.

As a matter of routine—serving both The Shadow and the *Classic*—Burke took a ride in his coupé and rolled past the old house where State police were on guard. His headlights, as they swerved, cut a swath of light across the front of the rambling mansion.

This time, the headlights revealed nothing. Yet they had actually uncovered a figure which Clyde Burke did not see.

After the reporter's car had rolled away, a soft, whispered tone of mockery sounded near the wall of the house. It was the laugh of The Shadow!

The master who solved crime had returned. His invisible shape edged toward the wall. It moved up the stone surface. It reached the window of the living room. One hand—The Shadow's right—raised the sash to form a narrow crevice.

Peering eyes saw the flicker of a fire in the grate. A State policeman was standing in the living room. As The Shadow watched, the officer strode away and went down the corridor.

The window opened farther. The Shadow entered. His sharp gaze turned toward the cupboard in the corner. Sulu's former abode had been opened by searchers. The door was wide; the cupboard was empty.

The Shadow, as he moved toward the corridor, showed the same swift precision that he had exhibited on his first visit to this house. As he sidled toward the wall, his right hand was at the front of his cloak; his left moved—rather slowly—at his side.

The Shadow had evidently recovered from the effects of the knife wound in his left arm, but he was also careful not to use too great effort. He reached the corridor and approached the panels at the side of the wall. The State policeman had gone downstairs.

The Shadow tried the panels. He raised one. His flashlight flickered through the long, narrow secret room. The Shadow threw the beams along the thick wall at the left. Then the light turned to the low ceiling just above his head. It remained there.

Returning to the corridor, The Shadow closed the panel. He ran his light along the corridor wall, past the next panel, then to the third. He opened this one. He entered the second secret room—the long, low, narrow chamber which was the counterpart of the first.

Again, the searching rays of the flashlight enabled The Shadow to make a thorough study of this room. A soft laugh resounded as The Shadow stepped back to the corridor and closed the secret panel. Slowly, with measured stride, he covered paces toward the first panel which he had opened. He stopped.

Someone was thumping up the stairs. With a swift whirl, The Shadow started for the living room. He arrived there just as a State policeman, on a tour of inspection, appeared at the head of the stairs.

When the officer arrived in the living room, The Shadow was no longer there. The master of darkness had returned into the depths of night. His presence, however, still remained in the neighborhood of the rambling mansion.

A swish—almost inaudible in the cool night air—announced The Shadow's arrival at the rear of the house.

The Shadow paused beside the shed which served as a garage. Beneath the heavy branches of a tree, the black-clad phantom climbed to the top of the outlying building.

From that spot, he gained the sloping roof of the mansion. Dull moonlight showed his form as a moving blot as it crept upward and reached the blackened side of the chimney. Clouds obscured the moon. Stygian darkness kept The Shadow unrevealed.

Half an hour passed. The Shadow's return was announced by a sighing whisper that came from the roof of the shed.

The Shadow had regained that spot after his unseen investigation. Silently, invisibly, the figure in black glided toward the side of the house. A State trooper, standing at the opened door of the mansion, was staring into the night. He did not see The Shadow.

The master of darkness had departed. His mission to the old house had been fulfilled. The Shadow, like Junius Tharbel, was playing a waiting game. He knew—The Shadow—that Mox, whoever he might be, still contemplated mischief.

One hour after The Shadow's mysterious departure, one of the State policemen heard a sound as he stood by the opened door. The noise seemed to come from the shed at the rear of the mansion.

The officer closed the door behind him. Cautiously, he stalked through the darkness. He heard the noise again—a grating on the roof of the shed.

Clicking his flashlight, the policeman raised his gun. The glare of the electric torch revealed a creature poised between the roof of the shed and the roof of the house.

Never before had the officer seen such an ugly monstrosity. The crooked dwarf, spreadeagled between the roofs, snarled furiously as the light showed his brownish face.

Writhing almost in mid-air, he shot back to the roof of the shed, just as the policeman fired his revolver. Sulu, unhit, disappeared over the other side of the shed.

The policeman ran around the low structure. He flashed his light in every direction. He saw no sign of the hideous monster.

Another policeman came running up. As he inquired what had happened, the first officer turned his flashlight upward as he heard a creaking limb. Poised upon the branch of the big tree was Sulu, about to attack the men below.

As the glare again disclosed his contorted form, the dwarf sprang downward, back toward the shed. Two revolvers thundered.

The intervening tree trunk saved Sulu as the shots were deflected. The long-limbed dwarf gained the shed; he bounded over its top and dropped between the small building and the house, while the officers again fired vain shots.

The policemen started in pursuit. Sulu, however, had gained the start. They arrived beside the house in time to discover the dwarf nearly a hundred feet away, making for a cluster of trees in a vacant patch of land.

Quick shots went wide. Sulu gained the safety spot he sought.

"Stay here," said one policeman, to his mate. "I'm going over to the nearest house and call the county detective."

People in the neighborhood had been aroused by the shots. Seeing the policeman beside the old house, in the glare from the now-opened door, they subsided. It was several minutes before the first officer returned.

"What did Tharbel have to say?" his companion inquired.

"That guy beats me," responded the officer who had telephoned. "He says he's not worried about prowlers. He also says that because we uncovered this funny-looking bird, we don't need another man on the job. He said that this afternoon; now he takes the attitude that this has proved it."

"Maybe he's right—but if that bimbo had plugged one of us from the tree, it wouldn't have looked so good."

"You bet it wouldn't!"

The State policemen continued their patrol. Keyed by the episode, they watched for a return of the prowler. The dwarf, however, did not appear near the house.

The watchers would have been amazed had they known that Mox's creature was not the first mysterious visitant who had been here this night. They had no inkling whatever of The Shadow's visit.

Where Sulu had been unsuccessful, spotted almost at the moment of his arrival, The Shadow had gained the objective which he sought. Yet Sulu, as well as the officers, was in ignorance of The Shadow's investigation.

71

Why had The Shadow come here tonight? What had brought Sulu to the premises, from which he had previously fled with Mox?

A partial answer to this question came later—in The Shadow's sanctum.

Located in his hidden abode, a black-walled apartment somewhere in Manhattan, The Shadow placed his long white hands beneath the bluish glare of the lamp that shone upon the polished table.

The Shadow held no trophy as a token of his trip to the old house in Darport. A sheet of paper—a pen—the sparkling girasol with its vivid flashes that turned from deep crimson to pure ultramarine—these were all that showed with The Shadow's hands.

The Shadow, however, had discovered something. It was locked within his brain. He was about to place his findings into words. The right hand raised the pen; upon the sheet of paper it inscribed two names:

Hoyt Wyngarth

Irving Salbrook

To date, neither of these men had figured in any of the reports that The Shadow had considered. There was nothing to show that they were henchmen of the fiend, or that they might be other missing inventors.

The names glared in vivid blue; then faded as though erased by an unseen hand. These were names which The Shadow had learned through his visit to the deserted home of Mox.

There was premonition in The Shadow's action. Although the names had disappeared, the men whom they represented were not forgotten. The Shadow had presaged their entry into the amazing case that involved Mox, the super-fiend.

The light clicked out. A laugh resounded in the gloom. Sardonic tones of merriment awoke taunting echoes that whispered sibilant notes from buried depths of blackness.

When the last gibe had ended, deep silence pervaded The Shadow's sanctum. The master of darkness had gone. His departure foretold the beginning of new and startling episodes.

The scheming of Mox had not yet ended. The Shadow had simply called the villain's next turn; and with it, The Shadow had marked the counterstroke which he—The Shadow—would deliver!

CHAPTER XII

CARDONA DRAWS A TRUMP

The morrow found Detective Joe Cardona impatiently pacing his office at headquarters. The star sleuth was in a grouchy mood. His trip to Darport had produced a tasteless aftermath.

Cardona picked up a newspaper; he read its front-page story. He threw the journal aside with a contemptuous snort. Angrily, he strode into another office, where he found the gray-haired inspector, Timothy Klein, seated at his desk.

Back on the job, Inspector Klein was taking matters easily after his long illness. He looked up as Cardona entered, noted the surly expression on the ace detective's face, and ventured a remark of inquiry.

"What's the matter, Joe?"

"Plenty, inspector," retorted the detective. "I go out to cooperate on a case, and a hick county detective tries to show me up for a sap."

"Hardly, Joe," rebuked Klein.

"I can't see it any other way," growled Cardona. "This has made me look like small change with the commissioner, I guess. Even the newspapers are taking a slam at me. Joe Cardona—ace of the New York force—trumped by a deuce! That's the way they're putting it. What's to be done about it?"

"Find a higher trump," suggested Klein.

"I'd like to do that!" blurted Cardona. "I'd like to make that guy Tharbel crawl. Say—the way he treated me! If he ever drives that old buggy of his down here—which I doubt, because it would fall apart five miles out of Darport—I'll have every traffic cop tipped to hand him a ticket."

Inspector Klein smiled. He felt that Cardona's anger was

exaggerated. Joe could become short-tempered at times. Nevertheless, Klein felt that the detective had cause for soreness. His visit to Darport had certainly not added to his prestige.

"The fox held out on me," declared Cardona emphatically. "He kept me guessing—that's all. I went up there because I was looking for a connection between Neswick and Greerson—both inventors. The newspapers brought it on; I followed it after I talked with the commissioner.

"I got the connection all right. But it wasn't the one I was looking for. I expected to find that Neswick and Greerson knew each other. Instead, I learned that Neswick, like Greerson, was a friend of Schuyler Harlew.

"See how that has twisted it? Moxton—or Mox as he called himself—is the murderer. He's the guy that got Harlew. He probably got Greerson. He was after Neswick. And all this while, I was looking for Greerson as a murderer. Who shows me I'm wrong? A hick detective, who holds back on the goods until he can make me look like a sap."

"Don't take it so tough, Joe."

"I wouldn't, if there was a way out. But the worst of it is that I've been trying to locate people whom Harlew knew. The only one I landed was Greerson—and he's gone. Along comes Junius Tharbel, big frog in a little puddle—and a muddy one, at that—to produce Neswick.

"Besides that, he has Neswick's testimony that Moxton was Harlew's boss. Say, inspector, this has got me buffaloed. I'm ready to quit—that's all. The newspapers have cut loose, and I'm a goat."

"Steady down, Joe," ordered Klein. "There'll be some breaks coming along pretty——"

"For Junius Tharbel, maybe," interposed Cardona. "He's a guy that plays for them. He can get them—in a bum town like Darport, where anybody that stays up after nine is probably a crook. If we had a curfew bell here in New York, I could round up a lot of thugs myself."

"There must be a way out."

"There is." Joe was emphatic as he spoke. "I'll tell you the kind of break I'd like to get, inspector. I found out about Greerson. I didn't know where he'd gone, but I know now that he went to Darport to see Mox.

"Tharbel puts me down as a sap by playing his trump. He gets Neswick. He brings the whole thing out. Neswick came to see Mox. The old gent tried to kill him. Murder is out in the open.

"What I'd like to get is a higher trump than Tharbel's. I'd like to find another inventor like Neswick—one who knew Schuyler Harlew—one who was going to see Mox—but one who hasn't started yet. That would be a trump card over Tharbel's. He thinks Neswick's testimony is O. K., and so do I. If I can play right down his alley, and bring in the kind of evidence he wants to——"

There was an interruption. Detective Sergeant Markham was at the door. He waved to Cardona.

"Fellow to see you, Joe," he said. "Wise-looking bloke. He's been reading the newspapers, and wants to talk to you about the Darport case——"

"Bring him in here," snorted Cardona.

"See?" This was to Inspector Klein. "Even Markham calls it the Darport case. Where do I rate?"

Before the inspector could reply, the visitor had arrived at the door of the office. Cardona and Klein found themselves facing a tall man whose erect posture and steady gaze marked him as an individual of intelligence. His features were the sharp ones that denoted a thinker. His manner was calm and dignified. In his early forties, this gentleman gave the impression of being one who had reached the prime of life.

"Detective Cardona?" inquired the visitor, in a mellow voice.

"Right," returned Joe. "Do you want to see me?"

"Yes." The man extended a card. Joe received it and read the name aloud: "Cuthbert Challick."

"Glad to meet you, Mr. Challick," expressed Cardona, extending his hand. "This is Inspector Klein."

Cardona noted the pressure of the gentleman's handshake. He was impressed by Challick's virility. The visitor, after shaking hands with Klein, calmly seated himself with the air of one who has an important story to tell.

"I have just returned to New York," began Challick. "I spend most of my time out of town; in Maine, Florida, and sometimes abroad. The first news that greeted me in the local newspapers was that of crime which began with the murder of one Schuyler Harlew, and ended with the flight of Jarvis Moxton—called Mox—from his home in Darport."

"I am handling the New York end of the case," interposed Cardona.

"So I understand," asserted Challick. "That is why I have

75

come to you. I am particularly interested in the testimony which the newspapers have attributed to a man named Joel Neswick. He, it appears, knew Harlew, and was told by Harlew to visit Mox. Am I correct?"

"Yes," replied Cardona. "Neswick is an inventor."

"So am I," declared Challick calmly. "I have been working on various inventions; some of them have proven profitable. My most recent experiments, however, have been with conical mirrors intended to gain heat power from the rays of the sun. My plans have reached the point of practicability.

"That, I suppose, is why I was visited by Schuyler Harlew, who made a special trip to Portland, Maine——"

"You knew Harlew?" Cardona blurted the question.

"Certainly," assured Challick. "I knew him only as the representative of a man who wished to purchase full rights to my invention——"

"Jarvis Moxton?"

"Mox, according to his own signature."

Drawing his hand from his inside pocket, Cuthbert Challick passed a folded note to Joe Cardona. The detective opened it. With eager eyes, he read:

Admit the bearer to my house. This will serve as his introduction.   Mox.

"You received this from Schuyler Harlew?" questioned Cardona, looking up from the scrawled lines.

"Yes," answered Challick. "More than a month ago. I promised to see Mox immediately upon my return to New York. I was to go to Darport after my arrival here. You can imagine my amazement to learn that Harlew had been murdered; that Mox was a fugitive from justice."

"I want you to go with me to Darport," announced Cardona.

"I am quite anxious to do so," agreed Challick. "This matter is of utmost importance to me. You must understand that I was assured a prompt purchase of my invention. I want to know what lies in back of it all."

"You'll learn," said Cardona grimly. "This is great news you've brought me, Mr. Challick."

Turning to Inspector Klein, the star detective brought his fist upon the desk with a resounding punch. There was triumph in Cardona's eyes.

"I've got the edge now, inspector!" he exclaimed. "I've got what Junius Tharbel needs—a man whose testimony will bear out what Neswick said; and one who has the proof which Neswick couldn't show—this note!"

Inspector Klein nodded.

"If this doesn't blast that wise hick loose," added Cardona, "I don't know what will! He thinks he showed me up; he's going to find out different. Tharbel trumped my ace; this time I'll cover his deuce spot."

Cardona turned to Cuthbert Challick. The tall inventor was looking on with an air that indicated perplexity. He seemed to be just on the verge of understanding the excited remarks that Cardona had uttered.

"We're going to Darport," announced Cardona. "You and I, Mr. Challick, to get the low-down on this crime."

Challick nodded his agreement. Cardona's swarthy features registered an elated smile.

The break had come in Cardona's favor. In Cuthbert Challick and the letter which the inventor had brought, the ace detective had gained the trump he wanted!

CHAPTER XIII

THARBEL COUNTERS

That same afternoon found Junius Tharbel seated at his rickety desk. The back window showed the county jail, the side window opened on a stretch of ground that was vacant for a distance of forty feet, beyond it a row of trees.

The gum-chewing county detective seemed to be awaiting the arrival of some one. Two reporters entered. They did not rouse Tharbel from his reverie.

Clyde Burke arrived.

"Hello, Tharbel," greeted the *Classic* reporter.

"Hello," returned the county detective. "Well, what do you want to ask me about? Let's hear it."

"No questions," said Clyde. "I don't ask them. If you have a statement, I'll listen to it."

Tharbel chuckled.

"You're all right, Burke," he said. "Just for that, I'll give you a statement. Get ready."

ing the arrival of someone. Two reporters entered. They crowded close to Tharbel's desk. The county detective arose solemnly and went to a closet. He brought forth a rifle and placed it on the desk.

"Nice Winchester, eh?" he questioned. "Well, here's my statement. I'm going hunting."

Clyde Burke laughed. The other reporters looked puzzled. Tharbel's hatchet-face formed a wry smile.

"Yes, sir," repeated the county detective. "I'm going hunting. Out to Hollis Harman's lodge. He and another fellow are coming here to get me. We start with the dogs at daybreak."

"What about Moxton?" questioned one of the reporters. "You're not dropping the case, are you? With somebody prowling around his house last night?"

"That's three questions," returned Tharbel sourly. "I don't have to answer any one of them. You heard my statement. I'm going hunting."

The hatchet-faced sleuth resumed his seat and stared idly from the window. It was a gloomy, fog-laden day. Dusk was settling. Tharbel, however, seemed indifferent to the weather. Departing from his usual custom, he became somewhat loquacious. Clyde Burke motioned to the other reporters to listen. The *Classic* representative knew Junius Tharbel's ways.

"I've been county detective for upward of twenty years," began Tharbel, in a reminiscent tone. "I've seen cases in my time; cases as tough as this one. It doesn't pay to let them throw you.

"I'm out to find a man who calls himself Jarvis Moxton. Mox. I'm not telling you anything you don't know when I say that name is phony. Jarvis Moxton does not exist. But there's someone—somewhere—who has been playing the part of an old man called Mox.

"He's gone from Darport, this murderer, Mox. He'll bob up some other place, and he'll get back here if we have to bring him. That's why I'm not saying much. That's why I'm waiting. That's why I'm going hunting."

The outside gloom seemed to increase while Tharbel delivered his slow, speculative tones. There was a confidence in the county detective's manner that proved impressive to the listeners.

"The break is due soon," resumed Tharbel. "You'll be seeing it—all three of you. Joel Neswick is staying here in Darport, to give his testimony when I want it. There'll be another witness, too——"

78

Tharbel broke off as if he had said enough. He swung back in his chair. He glanced toward the doorway.

"I guess Fatty Harman will be in from his lodge pretty soon," he remarked. "He'll pick up his friend, and they'll come to get me. Maybe I'll get some shooting in early to-morrow. There's murders and crime all the while, but the hunting season doesn't last long."

Footsteps began to clatter on the stairs. Tharbel arose and pointed to the single light which illuminated his office. He spoke to the reporters.

"Stick around if you want," he said. "If any phone calls come in, tell them I'm out at Harman's. If you go, the operator will know where to switch the calls. This sounds like my two friends."

At that moment, two men entered the office. A look of surprise appeared upon Tharbel's face; it changed to a challenge as the county detective recognized Joe Cardona.

The New York sleuth was accompanied by a tall, dignified man, who studied Junius Tharbel with a steady gaze. Joe Cardona, about to make the introduction, caught himself as he spied the reporters.

"I want to talk with you, Tharbel," was his greeting. "What I've got to say is important. If you don't want these reporters around——"

"It doesn't matter," interrupted Tharbel, with a tinge of sarcasm in his tone. "Whatever you've got to say, Cardona, can be said here. This isn't New York; it's Darport. However, if you want privacy, I'll arrange it for you."

Rising from his chair, the county detective marched to a door and opened it. He turned on the light in an adjoining room, as shabby as his regular office. He motioned to Cardona and his companion to enter.

Tharbel sat down at a desk as rattley as the one he usually used. Cardona, facing him squarely, answered his ironical challenge.

"If you don't mind the reporters," he declared, in a cold tone, "neither do I. If they're here to get a story, I'm willing to give it to them."

"Suits me," rejoined Tharbel.

"O. K." Cardona swung to the door of Tharbel's regular office. "Come in, boys. Here's something for your sheets."

Following Clyde Burke, the reporters flocked into the front room. Assuming a dramatic pose, Cardona began his

79

statement. Before introducing his companion, he set forth a quick résumé of the case on which he and Tharbel were working.

"A man named Schuyler Harlew," declared Cardona, "was murdered in New York. He knew an inventor named Peter Greerson, who disappeared.

"Then came Joel Neswick, another inventor. He showed up here in Darport, to keep an appointment with Jarvis Moxton—otherwise known as Mox. After Mox tried to kill Neswick, we got the story."

"I got it," interposed Tharbel.

"And I got it, too," returned Cardona, "after I talked with Neswick. Our theory, now, is that Greerson came here and was murdered. Neswick came here and was rescued. But don't forget one thing, Tharbel. The theory is based entirely upon Neswick's story."

"Yes," admitted Tharbel.

"Neswick says he had a note—a card of admittance to Mox."

"Yes."

"But he doesn't have it now. It went to Mox, from whom it had come, through Schuyler Harlew."

"Yes."

"All right," Cardona's voice rose triumphantly. "Only one thing is needed, Tharbel. That's further testimony to support what Neswick has said. Without it, Neswick's story can fall flat. Am I right?"

"I suppose so," admitted Tharbel cautiously.

"Can you produce such testimony?" demanded Cardona.

"No," replied Tharbel.

"Well, I can!" exclaimed Cardona. "I'll let the man speak in his own behalf.

"Gentlemen, this is Cuthbert Challick, an inventor, recently returned from Maine. I'll let him nail the clincher in his own words!"

All stared toward Challick. Even Junius Tharbel looked astounded for the moment. Cardona was elated. With arms folded, he listened while Challick spoke.

"Schuyler Harlew came to see me a month ago," announced Challick, in a firm, dignified voice. "In Portland, Maine, he requested me to visit a man named Jarvis Moxton, who lived in Darport. I agreed to do so, upon my return to New York. From Harlew, I received a note, to serve as introduction."

"A note signed by Mox!" blurted Cardona. "This is it!"

With a flourish, the ace detective planted the paper upon Tharbel's tumbledown desk. Reporters leaped forward to view it.

Tharbel studied the paper with apparent interest.

"This," he remarked, "will corroborate Neswick's story— provided, of course, that the note resembles Neswick's. It simply proves what I have learned——"

"What you have learned," snorted Cardona, "I have proven!"

The reporters looked at one another. Cardona saw their glances. He knew that credit was coming to him; that Tharbel's prestige was due for a jolt. The New York sleuth had brought the evidence that Tharbel needed.

The telephone bell rang in the other room. Methodically, Tharbel arose to answer it. When he returned, his face wore an expression of triumph that outshone Joe Cardona's.

"Give Cardona credit," said Tharbel, to the reporters. "He has brought in something useful. It is a corroboration —a written paper. In the meantime, I have not been idle. I, too, have gained a scrap of paper—a very useful one. I have it here. I shall read it."

He drew a scrawled slip from his pocket, and held it in the light. In a pauseless voice, he read these words:

"You want Mox. I can tell you where he is. In Albany. He calls himself Hoyt Wyngarth."

Tharbel planked the paper on the table. He faced the other men and smiled sourly. It was evident that he had another surprise to spring.

"This note," he said, "reached my hands last night. I sent a man to Albany to-day. The call that I just received was by long distance. I have been expecting it. Hoyt Wyngarth is a prisoner. He will arrive here to-morrow morning."

Junius Tharbel chuckled gloatingly as he looked at Joe Cardona. The New York ace had played a trump; he had brought a new and useful witness. But the county detective had countered with a dazzling thrust.

He, Junius Tharbel, had accomplished the important result. He had brought about the arrest of a suspect who might be Mox himself!

CHAPTER XIV

THE SHADOW ENTERS

Junius Tharbel relished his triumph over Joe Cardona. While the New York detective and the reporters stared at the scrawled sheet upon the table, Tharbel stood back and watched them, triumph in his eyes.

The note was exactly as Tharbel had read it. The words, though crudely written, were legible. Cardona noted something which Tharbel had not stated. The note was signed with a single letter—"S."

"Where did you get this?" challenged Cardona.

"Where did you get your note?" queried Tharbel.

"It was brought into my office," retorted Cardona. "By the man who is here with me—Cuthbert Challick."

"Well," chuckled Tharbel, "my note was delivered at my home. Unfortunately, the man who left it did not stay. I found it wedged under the door."

"A hoax."

"We shall see. I have a test."

Cardona suddenly remembered the coach dog that Tharbel had found in the house of Mox. Yes, the county detective had a test; one that he could use when Hoyt Wyngarth was brought in to-morrow. If the dog should recognize Wyngarth as its master!

"Suppose"—Tharbel was making a bland suggestion—"that we communicate with Neswick at the inn. He would like to meet Mr. Challick. You and I, Cardona, can compare the statements of the two."

Tharbel's tone was one of quiet conciliation. He had bettered the New York sleuth. He wanted cooperation. Cardona had nothing to do but agree.

"All right," he said, in a surly tone. "Call up Neswick. Let's talk to him."

Tharbel arose and walked into the other office. Cardona, Challick, and the reporters followed him. Challick partly closed the door to the front office. The paper which Tharbel had exhibited was still upon the desk.

Tharbel telephoned. He received word that Neswick was out for a walk with Scudder. The two were expected to return at any minute. The county detective settled complacently in his chair. Cardona sat down close by the desk.

One of the reporters went out for cigarettes. Challick, opening an ornamental case, found that he had but two of his own. Apparently following the reporter's lead, he strolled from the office also.

Minutes went slowly by. Silence reigned as the men in Tharbel's office awaited word from Joel Neswick. There was a motion in the hallway; no one observed it. The door of the front office—not the connecting one, but a portal that led to the outer hall—opened softly.

A figure in black entered. It was The Shadow. Stealing swiftly, the phantom glided to the connecting door and peered through the crack which remained.

He viewed Tharbel and Cardona; Clyde Burke and another reporter. Cardona, recovered from his gloom, had just begun to speak.

"So you landed a suspect, eh?" he questioned. "Who is this Hoyt Wyngarth?"

"A man we located in Albany," returned Tharbel brusquely. "That's all we know."

"Well"—Cardona's tone was doubtful—"I hope he's Mox. Good luck to you, Tharbel, but you can't place too much reliance in notes that come under your front door."

"Perhaps not," admitted Tharbel, with a slow smile.

Silence in the rear room. The Shadow glided away from the connecting door. His sharp eyes glittered as they looked about the front office.

The Shadow approached the desk and studied the note upon the table. A pile of blank sheets of paper lay close by. The Shadow scorned them. Instead, he drew a thinner sheet from beneath his cloak, and laid it on the table.

With a pencil, he copied the note which Tharbel had received. Word for word—with notable exceptions. Instead of Albany, he wrote New York. Instead of Hoyt Wyngarth, he put in the name of Irving Salbrook.

The work was craftily performed. The handwriting of The Shadow so closely resembled the original scrawl that not even an expert could have detected any difference.

The Shadow did not touch the note upon the table. He placed his own sheet of paper beneath his cloak, and disappeared through the door to the hall. The swish of his black garments was inaudible. He disappeared into the darkness of the stairs.

A few minutes later, Cuthbert Challick came up the steps. He was smoking a cigarette. He pointed to the slot machines lined up along the wall as he entered.

"The reporter is playing one of those," he remarked. "Over in the cigar store across the street. By the way"—he was turning to Cardona—"I sent those bags that we left at the store over to the inn. I thought we would probably be staying here all night."

"Of course." It was Tharbel who spoke, not Cardona. "You want to be here, Mr. Challick, when we quiz this prisoner Wyngarth. Your statements may prove of great value."

Tharbel, for the first time, remembered the note that he had left in the other room. He arose and hurried through the door. He brought back the paper that bore Hoyt Wyngarth's name, and thrust it in a drawer of his desk.

New footsteps on the stairs. Two men came in. They were carrying rifles. Tharbel arose to greet one of them, a pudgy, fat-faced fellow, who wore a perpetual smile.

"Hello, Harman!" he exclaimed. "Ready to go out to the lodge?"

"Sure thing," returned the fat-faced fellow. "Meet my friend, Wade Hosth. Just met him up at the inn. I was late. Hosth thinks he's a good shot. You can show him what shooting is to-morrow."

Junius Tharbel shook hands with a tall, sad-faced man, who was the exact contrast of Hollis Harman. He turned and introduced the pair of arrivals to Joe Cardona and Cuthbert Challick.

"I guess Neswick's not back at the inn yet," Tharbel remarked. "Well, that doesn't matter. It's only a block down there. You're staying overnight. Why don't you go down and meet him there? It's more comfortable than here."

"Aren't you going to record Mr. Challick's complete statement?" questioned Cardona, in surprise.

"You've got it, haven't you?" returned Tharbel abruptly. "I've got Neswick's; you've got Challick's. Scudder is over there. He can attend to the details.

"I'm shooting early to-morrow. They're bringing Wyngarth in, and I'll have to be here before noon. I'm going to

84

eat and sleep. I've got to keep in trim, you know. In New York"—Tharbel was grinning as he looked at Cardona—"you've got open season all the year around. You can bag gangsters any time you want. But out here, it's different. We get rusty if we miss the hunting when we have it."

With this sally, Junius Tharbel picked up his rifle and departed with Hollis Harman and Wade Hosth. Joe Cardona looked at Cuthbert Challick. The inventor shook his head and smiled.

"Let's go over to the inn," suggested Cardona.

Followed by Clyde Burke and the other reporter, the two from New York left the offices. Clyde, as an afterthought for Junius Tharbel's negligence, turned out the light. He saw a gleam from the front office and extinguished the light there also. He swung the doors shut. Their spring locks clicked.

Complete gloom pervaded the room in which The Shadow had performed the strange mission of imitating the note which Junius Tharbel had shown to Joe Cardona.

One note—that named Hoyt Wyngarth—had reached the hands of the county detective. The other—naming Irving Salbrook—remained in The Shadow's possession.

Hoyt Wyngarth and Irving Salbrook. These men were unknown factors. One had been thrust into the picture of crime. The other was absent—would be absent—until The Shadow should choose to deliver the note that he had prepared.

CHAPTER XV

THE TEST

Morning found Detective Joe Cardona at the county jail. The New York sleuth was anxious to witness the arrival of Hoyt Wyngarth from Albany.

The event took place shortly before noon.

An automobile pulled up in front of the jail. Two men alighted from the front, three from the rear, of the sedan. Hoyt Wyngarth, handcuffed between two captors, was led into the prison.

Cardona watched the man go by. Wyngarth, tall, stoop-shouldered, and cadaverous, looked pale and miserable. He was conducted to a cell. Cardona talked with the men who had brought him. Three were from Albany; the fourth, who had driven the car, was one of Tharbel's assistant detectives.

"He won't talk," affirmed one of the Albany sleuths. "We've got plenty on him, though. He's been suspected of blackmail a couple of times. A bad egg, this bird Wyngarth, and a smooth one."

"He doesn't look so smooth," remarked Joe.

"He's scared—that's why," rejoined the dick from Albany. "I guess he knows the clamps are on him."

Tharbel's assistant was calling Harman's hunting lodge. He announced, when he had completed his telephone conversation, that Junius Tharbel would arrive at the jail within a short time.

"He wants you to be here," the man told Cardona, "and he said to bring a fellow named Challick. I'm calling the inn to get Scudder and Neswick."

"Challick is with them."

"All right. I'll get the three over."

The trio arrived; with Cardona, they waited in the gloomy hallway just within the door of the jail. Tharbel showed up not long afterward. Accompanied by his hunting companions, Hollis Harman and Wade Hosth, he stalked into the hallway.

Reporters, too, were on the job. They strolled into the place in Tharbel's wake. The county detective raised no objection to their presence. With a curt nod to Cardona and the others, Tharbel walked through the hallway and opened the door of a side room.

"Come in here," he ordered.

Everyone obeyed. They found a room which had evidently been disused. It was separated, by a glass-framed partition, from a smaller room beyond it. All the windows had bars; there was a connecting door between the two.

"This layout," declared Tharbel, "was supposed to be my office. One of the county prosecutors rigged it up after the addition had been built to the jail. I was supposed to sit in there"—he pointed to the other room as he spoke—"and have my assistants out here. I tried it, barred windows and all, and then I moved back to my old offices. The prosecutor was sore, but we've had a new one since then."

Tharbel was unusually loquacious. It was seldom that he spoke at such lengths. He paused to smile sourly as he came to the point of his remarks.

"I've been figuring for a long while what I could do with these vacant rooms," he said. "At last, I've found a use for them. Pull down those shades, Scudder. I'm going to make a dark room out of this one."

Scudder obeyed. The darkening of the room produced a gloom that was lightened only by the illumination which came through the clear glass partition.

"Line up along the partition, all of you," ordered Tharbel. "Keep back far enough so your faces won't show from the other side."

The crowd followed instructions. Cardona took a position beside Challick and Neswick. Tharbel's hunting companions were next; on the other side of the door were Burke and the reporters who had come with him.

Tharbel opened the door in the partition, and went into the next room. He looked at the faces along the glass. He called out for the reporters to move back a bit. Satisfied, he put his head through the door and spoke:

"I'm going to quiz Hoyt Wyngarth. I'll leave the door open a little way, so you can hear as well as see. No noise. Understand? I'm coming in here later, and leave Wyngarth alone. No noise then, either."

Speaking in an undertone to Scudder, Tharbel gave new instructions. The assistant went out. Tharbel returned to the lighted office. As he promised, he left the door a trifle ajar. Tharbel seated himself in a chair.

The watchers saw a door open on the other side of the lighted room. Hoyt Wyngarth, relieved from his handcuffs, entered. The county detective invited him to sit down. The grilling was to begin.

Joe Cardona, watching and listening, again felt admiration as well as disapproval for Tharbel's methods. There was no challenge of the third degree in the county detective's manner. Tharbel was calm, almost friendly toward Wyngarth. At the same time, he was enigmatic; his hatchet-face showed no expression.

"What's your name?" questioned Tharbel quietly.

"Hoyt Wyngarth," blurted the pale-faced man.

"You live in Albany, eh?"

"Yes."

"Ever been in Darport before?"

"No."

Wyngarth's face, twitching, became suddenly tense as the prisoner made the final reply.

"That's odd," decided Tharbel. "I thought that maybe you knew something about a man who used to live in Darport. He called himself Mox—short for Moxton—Jarvis Moxton."

"I don't know him."

"Mox was the man's assumed name. Mox might be anyone. For instance"—Tharbel paused to smile for the first time—"I, myself, might be Mox. You might be Mox. The man, as he was known here, was a masquerader. Gray hair—gray beard—all probably false."

Wyngarth winced. His face, however, became suddenly firm after that. He seemed quite determined to say nothing.

"Do you want to answer questions?" queried Tharbel. "Or do you prefer to make a statement?"

"Neither," replied Wyngarth. "I have nothing to say. Nothing."

"Sure of that?"

"Yes."

Tharbel arose and strolled about the room. He started toward the far door, and paused to open the wrapper of a stick of chewing gum. As he used his right hand to place the gum in his mouth, he placed his left upon the knob and gave it a slight turn. Then, as an afterthought, he walked straight across the room and opened the door to the front room, where the hidden watchers were located.

"I'll be back," he promised, as he went through. He closed the door until only a crack remained. He joined those who were at the partition.

Hoyt Wyngarth, alone, stared solemnly toward the door by which Tharbel had left. He looked about in a furtive manner, noted the barred windows. He again faced the door between the two rooms.

The watchers, looking beyond, saw the farther door open. A big-fisted jailer stooped and shoved a dog into the room. Stepping back, he pulled the door shut.

The growl of the dog, the slam of the door; both attracted Wyngarth's attention. Turning, the prisoner—like the watchers—saw the brown-spotted Dalmatian that had been captured in Mox's upstairs living room.

Wyngarth gasped. The dog, still growling, stared at the

88

man. Then, with sudden recognition, the Dalmatian sprang toward Hoyt Wyngarth. Its growl turned to a yelp of joy.

As Wyngarth backed away, the dog leaped and pressed its paws against his body. With wagging tail, it looked to Wyngarth as any hound would welcome a long-lost master.

Wyngarth's reactions were a medley. For a moment, he forgot himself. Though backing away, he began to stroke the head of his canine friend. Then, with anger, he thrust the dog away, and sprang toward the door in the partition.

"Take the dog away!" he screamed. "Take it away! I'm afraid of it!"

Tharbel shut the door tight and held the knob. Wyngarth, the dog bounding after him, dashed across the room toward the farther door. As he fumbled with the knob, the Dalmatian, with tail wagging furiously, again showed its recognition.

The door opened. The beefy jailer pushed Wyngarth aside. As Tharbel, calling from the partition, gave him an order, the jailer grabbed the dog and pulled it from the room. The dog snarled at the jailer.

Wyngarth had collapsed in a chair. He looked up to see Junius Tharbel facing him. The county detective had entered the room after the removal of the dog.

"It looks like the hound knew you," he remarked.

"I never saw the dog before," whined Wyngarth.

"The dog knew you," reminded Tharbel. "He took to you, and no one else."

Wyngarth was silent.

"The dog," added Tharbel, "belonged to Mox."

Wyngarth clenched his fists, and cowered in his chair. His eyes were wild as they stared toward Tharbel.

"I've got nothing to say!" shrieked the prisoner. "Nothing! Nothing!"

"Very well." Tharbel seemed indifferent. "We'll keep you as our guest for a while, and see how you enjoy it."

The county detective called for Scudder. The assistant arrived. Tharbel ordered him to take Wyngarth back to a cell. The prisoner became defiant as he was being led from the room.

"I'll never talk!" he cried.

"No?" questioned Tharbel. "Well, we'll find out about that. Remember, Wyngarth, any time that you are ready to make a statement, you can do so. Simply ask to be brought to me. I'll be glad to see you."

There was a quiet impressiveness about Tharbel's statement. The words had their effect upon Wyngarth. The tall man's stooped shoulders seemed to sag as the men swung him through the hallway. Tharbel beckoned to the men who had been patiently standing beyond the door.

"That's that," he said, as the crowd entered the room which contained daylight. "I've landed the man I want. When Hoyt Wyngarth confesses, we'll know all there is to know about Mox."

"Aren't you going to grill him?" demanded Joe Cardona.

"I have completed my examination of the prisoner," returned Tharbel. "When he talks, it will be of his own volition. He will send for me."

Turning about, Tharbel spied his fat-faced friend Hollis Harman and the hunter's companion, Wade Hosth. He beckoned to the pair.

"Let's get started," he suggested. "We'll go back and do some shooting. Scudder"—this to the assistant who had just returned—"when Wyngarth wants to talk, send for me. I'll be staying out at the lodge."

Joe Cardona stood rooted for a full minute after Junius Tharbel had departed with his friends. When the detective turned about, he found himself with a trio consisting of Cuthbert Challick, Joel Neswick, and Scudder. The reporters had followed after Junius Tharbel.

"This beats me," growled Joe. "Tharbel gets the goods on a guy, then won't try to make him talk."

"That's his way," interposed Scudder. "I've seen him try it before. I guess he figures that the prisoner will worry himself until he weakens."

"Well," remarked Neswick, with a smile, "that keeps me over at the inn for a while longer. I can't say that I mind it. Let's go over and have lunch, Scudder."

The two men went out. Joe Cardona was alone with Cuthbert Challick. The detective turned to the tall inventor.

"There's no reason why you've got to stay," remarked Joe. "You've made your statement. You're not a material witness. I'm going to stay out here until Hoyt Wyngarth talks. If you'll let me know where you will be in New York——"

90

"I think I shall remain here," interposed Challick. "This case is becoming very interesting. Tharbel's dog test was good—so far as it went. Yes, I shall stay in Darport for a few days at least. Suppose we go over and join Neswick at lunch."

"I'll be along in a few minutes," said Cardona, as they walked from the room. "I want to talk with these fellows who brought Wyngarth in from Albany."

Outside the jail, Cardona found the men he wanted. He saw Challick's tall form strolling toward the inn as he talked with the Albany detectives. As Challick disappeared from view, something that an Albany man said aroused Cardona from his lethargy.

"Tharbel is smart," was the comment. "He grabs Wyngarth. The dog knows the guy. You can't beat that. I'd like to see somebody else pull one as smooth as that."

Cardona thrust his hands in his pocket. He stalked away. Growling as he walked toward the inn, he expressed his antagonism toward Junius Tharbel.

"Thought he was smart," grunted Joe. "Found Neswick. I trumped that when I found Challick. He's overplayed me now—with that note naming Wyngarth. The dog knows Wyngarth, all right.

"Say"—Cardona stopped short, and his lips moved as he spoke to himself, half aloud—"if I could get a break like that! Find a guy that the dog would recognize! That would make Tharbel look cheap!"

Something crinkled as Cardona clenched his fist within his pocket. Wondering, the detective brought out a crumpled sheet of paper. His eyes bulged as he read the scrawl that ended with the signed letter "S."

Cardona, like Tharbel, had gained possession of a mysterious note. Like the message which Cardona had seen on Tharbel's desk, this one began with the words: "You want Mox——"

But instead of Hoyt Wyngarth, in Albany, it named Irving Salbrook, in New York!

A grim smile spread over Cardona's features. The sleuth saw the opportunity.

The letter "S." Who it meant, Cardona did not know. But he held a lurking thought that the letter had a double meaning now. To Cardona, "S" signified The Shadow!

He was sure that the mysterious stranger who moved by stealth had thrust his amazing hand into the affairs that surrounded the affairs of Mox, the superfiend.

When he reached the inn, Cardona went to a telephone before he joined the others at lunch. He called New York detective headquarters, and talked with Inspector Timothy Klein. All arrangements were made to snag Irving Salbrook, if he could be located in New York.

Junius Tharbel had applied the test on Hoyt Wyngarth. Joe Cardona had a hunch that he, too, would have occasion to soon apply the same test on another prisoner.

CHAPTER XVI

CARDONA'S TEST

At dusk the next day, a coupé pulled up in front of Hollis Harman's hunting lodge. From the car stepped Detective Joe Cardona. Clyde Burke clambered from the driver's seat. The detective had arranged with the reporter to bring him to this place. He wanted Clyde Burke to be on hand to see what might develop.

Cardona knocked. The door of the lodge opened. The detective strode into a large room where he found Junius Tharbel seated before a fire with his host, and Harman's friend, Wade Hosth. The three showed surprise when they recognized the New Yorker.

"What brings you here, Cardona?" inquired Tharbel.

"Something that will interest you," returned Joe. "Some time ago, you received a note signed 'S'—and it enabled you to capture Hoyt Wyngarth. I want to ask you a question. Was the note the only reason for the test that you gave to Wyngarth?"

"The test with the Dalmatian? Certainly. The dog's response proved that the sender of the note had given me reliable information."

"All right. Was that the only note you received?"

"With the signature of 'S'? Certainly. Why should there have been another, after Mox had been betrayed?"

"There is a second note," rejoined Cardona, "but you did not receive it. The note came to me. Here it is."

Cardona pulled the paper from his pocket, and handed it

to Tharbel. The county detective frowned as he read the scrawled lines. He passed it back to Cardona.

"A hoax," he declared. "Someone playing a joke on you, Cardona. When did you get this? Where?"

"Never mind the questions," retorted Cardona, with a grim smile. "I saw your note; this one resembles it in every detail. It's not a fake."

"We can compare them to-morrow," announced Tharbel, in a matter-of-fact tone. "I intend to stop in at my offices. If you bring your note there, we can lay it along with the one that I received."

"I'm not thinking of to-morrow," challenged Joe. "I'm thinking of to-day. What are you going to do about this fellow, Irving Salbrook? Try to grab him?"

"There would be no purpose in that," returned Tharbel, with a shrug of his shoulders "I have satisfied myself that Wyngarth is the dog's master. Wyngarth must be Mox. Give him time, and he'll confess. Why cloud it by going on a blind trail?"

"So that's the way you feel about it," snorted Cardona. "There's a story for you, Burke. Junius Tharbel refuses to apply the famous coach-dog test to a new suspect. He's out to frame Hoyt Wyngarth——"

"Don't print that!" shouted Tharbel angrily, as he leaped to his feet. "I never said that I would not use the dog for another identification. Cardona wants me to start after a fake suspect. Why should I bother to do so? Let him find this Irving Salbrook if he wants. When he brings him to Darport, I'll let the dog see the man."

"You will?" Cardona's query showed triumph to come. "That's just what I've come to learn. If I bring in Salbrook——"

"I'll give him the dog test, any time you ask it."

"Great." Joe Cardona grinned. "We'll start for the county jail right now, Tharbel. Detective Sergeant Markham arrived on the last train with Irving Salbrook accompanying him as his prisoner."

Dumfoundment spread over Tharbel's sharp features. Cardona's declaration had stumped the county detective. He saw that Clyde Burke sided with Cardona; when he stared toward Hollis Harman and Wade Hosth, he saw that his hunting friends were of a similar mind.

"A sporting proposition, Tharbel!" exclaimed the fat-faced host. "By Jove! That's fair enough. Cardona has brought the suspect here——"

"And if the dog recognizes Salbrook," interrupted Cardona, speaking to Tharbel, "you can keep the man along with Wyngarth."

There was nothing for Tharbel to do but agree to these terms. The county detective realized that the test with Wyngarth would not stand if he were unwilling to try the dog with others. Reluctantly, he donned hat and coat, and motioned to his friends to come along.

People were awaiting them at the jail. Scudder was there, with Joel Neswick and Cuthbert Challick. Cardona announced that Markham was in the warden's room, guarding Irving Salbrook.

Without a word, Junius Tharbel drew the shades of the front room where he had formerly stationed watchers. He turned on the lights in the rear room of the pair, and extinguished the lights in the front.

Behind the blackened glass of the partition, the gallery looked on to view the approaching test. Tharbel appeared in the smaller room. A few minutes later, Markham arrived, bringing Irving Salbrook from the rear entrance.

The new prisoner was not quite so tall as Hoyt Wyngarth. He wore the same hunted expression, however, and his face was pale. He seemed to be as determined a type of man.

He glowered as he faced Tharbel. The county detective applied a few quiet questions.

"I don't know anything about Darport," retorted Salbrook, in answer to a query. "Never heard of the burg before."

"And Mox?"

"I don't know anything at all about him."

Tharbel reported the actions that he had used with Wyngarth. With spectators watching him, and Joe Cardona demanding a fair trial, the county detective went to the further door and signaled with the knob. He crossed the room, entered the front apartment, and waited with the others.

Salbrook glared suspiciously. He heard the further door click. He scowled as the brown-spotted dog was shoved into the room. He showed his antagonism at once.

"Get away, hound!" he shouted. "Get away!"

At the sound of Salbrook's voice, the Dalmatian looked up. With a happy yelp, it bounded across the room, and began to paw Salbrook as it had pawed Wyngarth. The man fought with the beast, but to no avail. The dog's

94

endeavors to be friendly merely made the recognition more emphatic.

The jailer hurried in when Tharbel called from the dark room. He dragged the dog away. Its growls commenced as soon as the jailer had taken charge.

Salbrook sat panting in a chair. Tharbel opened the door when the dog was gone. With Cardona, he entered to take charge of Salbrook.

"You're going to hold this man," said Cardona, as though taking it for granted.

Tharbel nodded. He ordered Scudder to take the prisoner to a cell. Irving Salbrook was led away.

Joe Cardona was triumphant. Tharbel, however, took some of the edge from the New Yorker's elation.

"I'll treat Salbrook exactly like I'm treating Wyngarth," asserted the county detective. "Wyngarth was brought in from Albany; Salbrook from New York. That's the only difference. If either one wants to talk, he can. But there'll be no third degree. I don't work that way."

"Salbrook was hooked up with some rackets in New York," explained Cardona. "We haven't got anything on him—enough to matter—but Markham didn't have any trouble grabbing him. He was easy to locate, once we had his name."

"Come over to my office," suggested Tharbel. "I want to look at the note I have there."

When they reached the county detective's office, Tharbel opened the desk drawer and brought out the note which he said had been found beneath the front door of his home. Cardona laid his note on the desk. The comparison indicated that they must have been written by the same person.

Tharbel was rubbing his chin in a perplexed fashion. Seeing that the county detective was apparently at a loss about the matter, Cardona propounded his theory.

"One of these fellows may be Mox," he asserted. "Maybe the other was a friend he got the dog from. Some guy may be sore at them both."

The theory was weak, but Junius Tharbel did not criticize it. He seemed to be considering a countermove now that Cardona had triumphed. The rivalry between the two detectives had reached its highest pitch. When Tharbel did speak, it was to choose the easiest way out of the dilemma.

"Wyngarth is due to talk soon," he commented. "When he does, we'll know the story. There's nothing to do until the break comes."

The county detective arose from his desk and turned to Hollis Harman and Wade Hosth, who were standing within the door. There was a note of decision in the words that Tharbel spoke.

"Let's start back to the lodge," he said. "We'll need some sleep to-night. We'll be starting out with the dogs at daybreak."

Chapter XVII

DEATH INTERRUPTS

The following afternoon found Joe Cardona at the county jail. The New York ace had taken it upon himself to watch affairs there, even though his capacity was ex officio. If Junius Tharbel preferred to go hunting when he should be grilling prisoners, that did not relieve Cardona from the duty which he felt was his lot.

Somehow, Cardona had a hunch that a break was coming soon. He mentioned the fact to Clyde Burke and Cuthbert Challick, both of whom were with him, but he did not state the underlying reason for his hunch.

"There's something phony about the way Tharbel is acting," was Cardona's chief declaration. "Maybe he knows more than he says; that's the only answer I can figure out."

It was not Tharbel's part, however, that weighed so heavily in the formation of Cardona's hunch. The New York sleuth was positive that another figured in this case; one whose power was sure to be felt ere long. Cardona was thinking of The Shadow.

Knowing The Shadow's ability at crime detection, realizing that The Shadow was also a master of disguise, Cardona was sure that the master investigator had been present at important events.

He was sure that The Shadow had witnessed the dog

tests, particularly the first, for it was after that occurrence that Cardona had found the note that pointed to Irving Salbrook.

Consideration had enabled Cardona to analyze the game, even though he could not place the participants as he wished. The inclusion of The Shadow made Cardona's analysis hold water.

It was evident, first of all, that Mox must be matching his wits against the law. The superfiend had disappeared, yet Cardona felt that he was still present, playing an important part.

The note naming Hoyt Wyngarth could well have been supplied by Mox. The villain's plan was to shift his identity onto a man who for some reason feared to speak.

The Shadow had countered Mox's move. He had enabled Cardona, through a second note, to uncover Irving Salbrook. That had temporarily shattered the case against Hoyt Wyngarth.

Although Junius Tharbel did not seem to like it, Hoyt Wyngarth had actually been cleared of the threatening suspicion which surrounded him. Irving Salbrook now shared the burden which had originally rested upon Wyngarth.

Either of the two could be Mox; and with two possible claimants at hand, it was even more logical that neither man was Mox.

Mox!

The name maddened Cardona. He felt that Mox was clever enough to be in this game, throwing the mechanism of the law out of kilter. By posing as a person interested in the case, the man of murder had many opportunities to cover his evil trail.

The Shadow!

There was the gleam of hope. He, too, was clever. Cardona was sure that The Shadow was playing the part of an individual who had some interest in the case, and that he—the master of detection—was breaking down the barriers that Mox was setting.

Cardona could do nothing but wait and let the atmosphere clear. It might take days, but the star detective hoped that the break would be soon. That was why he stayed about the jail, and even while Cardona waited idly, the break arrived.

It was the local jailer who brought the news. Cardona

saw the beefy man at the door. He approached as the jailer beckoned. Clyde Burke and Cuthbert Challick followed.

"This guy Wyngarth is gone cuckoo," announced the jailer. "Walking about his cell like a caged lion. He wants to talk. Says he's got to see Tharbel."

"Get Tharbel," said Cardona quickly.

"I've called the hunting lodge," returned the jailer. "They're out shooting. A car has gone out to look for them. Meanwhile Wyngarth is getting wild."

"Call Scudder," suggested Cardona.

"Say!" The idea hit the jailer as he spoke. "That's a good idea. Sure thing—Scudder's over at the inn, ain't he? I'll tell him to come here."

The call was made. Three minutes later, Scudder appeared with Neswick. The trouble was explained. Scudder beckoned as he started for Wyngarth's cell.

The prisoner appeared pitiable. He was clutching the bars of the cell door, staring through with pale face pressed against the metal. His lips were parched. His voice was hoarse.

"I can't stand it!" he shrieked, as he saw the people who arrived. "I'm afraid—afraid—afraid——"

Scudder did not know what to say. Joe Cardona, noting the hesitation of Tharbel's assistant, took it upon himself to assume charge.

"You'd better talk, Wyngarth," he declared.

"I've been afraid to talk!" Wyngarth's tone was pleading. "I've been afraid—because I know what will happen if I do talk. But I'm going to break—it's coming—and the sooner I chance it, the better I'll be."

"Tell us about it."

"Not here! Not here!" Wyngarth screamed. "Take me away from this cell—away from this jail. I'll tell all I know! But don't leave me, now that I've promised to speak. You can't leave me!"

Convulsive sobs came from Wyngarth's throat. The listeners stared solemnly. They knew that Wyngarth's fears were real.

"We've sent for Tharbel," assured Cardona. "He'll be coming in here shortly. He'll take you to his office. He'll let you talk."

"I can't wait!" wailed Wyngarth. "If I wait, I'll lose my nerve! I won't talk—ever—if you don't hear me now. I can't talk in this place. Unless you get me out of here——"

"How about it?" questioned Cardona, turning to Scudder. "Why not take him up to Tharbel's office? You have a key, haven't you?"

"Yes," admitted Scudder, "but Tharbel has left orders to keep Wyngarth in here."

"Perhaps," returned Cardona testily, "but Tharbel ought to be around. I've seen cases like this before. When a man wants to talk, you've got to take advantage of it."

"Something may happen to me," pleaded Wyngarth. "I'd talk here, if I dared. But these bars frighten me. I'll be freed after I tell my story. Take me out of here!"

He began to rattle the bars furiously as he spoke. There was no question about Wyngarth's highly nervous condition. Joe Cardona saw that much could be gained by removing him at once.

"Tharbel's a fine guy," growled Cardona. "Thinks he's the big boss of this county. No one can make a move without his permission——"

"What about the county prosecutor?" The subtle suggestion came from Cuthbert Challick, who was standing by.

"You've hit it!" exclaimed Cardona. "He's over Tharbel! Where's his office, Scudder?"

"Down the street," was the reply. "He should be there now."

"I'll get him," decided Cardona, in a grim tone, as he left the cell room.

Five minutes afterward, Joe Cardona returned, accompanied by a squat, gray-haired man. This was Barry Davies, the county prosecutor. Scudder approached as the official arrived.

"Hello, prosecutor," he said. "This fellow Wyngarth wants to make a confession. He won't talk while he's in his cell. He says he can't wait to talk."

"Tharbel is out hunting, eh?" questioned the prosecutor.

"Yes," returned Scudder. "We've sent for him."

The prosecutor looked at Wyngarth. The prisoner began a new plea, in a sincere, quieted tone.

"I'm worried here," he explained. "I've heard—I've seen"—he threw a quick glance over his shoulder toward the barred window of his cell—"well, I can't tell you my fears until I'm somewhere safe. Somewhere above ground, where I'm free to talk——"

"I never like to interfere with Tharbel," interposed the prosecutor. "He is a highly competent man. Interference

99

only destroys his work. I would prefer to keep this man in his cell until Tharbel arrives."

"This is an emergency," insisted Cardona.

"I know that," nodded the prosecutor. "Therefore, I am willing to depart from my customary policy. Everything must be done in precise fashion. Scudder, you can bring the prisoner to Tharbel's office. I shall have a court stenographer present to take down his statement."

A sigh of relief came from Hoyt Wyngarth's lips. Then, with glowing eyes, the prisoner spoke to the prosecutor.

"I'll tell you everything," he promised. "About the dog, too—why he knows me. You can bring the dog there. Let me see him. I'm sorry I treated him the way I did when he was thrust into the room where I was. Poor old fellow! He's my friend!"

The prosecutor was doubtful. Finally, he made another decision of approval.

"Have the dog taken to the front office of Tharbel's suite," he ordered. "Wyngarth to the rear office—the regular one. Wait a moment—let me see whom I'll admit there."

He glanced at the faces of those about him. Joe Cardona supplied the introductions.

"Clyde Burke, reporter of the New York *Classic,*" said the sleuth. "This man is Joel Neswick, who was rescued from the old house. This is Cuthbert Challick, whom I brought from New York to testify that he had been asked to visit Mox——"

"All right," nodded the prosecutor. "These men will be admitted."

The group broke up. As they were leaving the cell room so that Scudder could take the prisoner alone, they heard Hoyt Wyngarth babble wildly.

"Guard me!" were his words. "I'm being watched! There will be danger when I'm outside! Please be careful. Mox is a fiend!" It was the first time that Wyngarth had uttered the monster's name. "Mox has creatures who do his bidding! I know that one of them must be near!"

Scudder and the jailer took charge of Wyngarth. They did not bring the prisoner through the front. They whisked him out by a side entrance, into a back door of the building which contained Tharbel's offices and up the stairs.

Sultry dusk was settling around the buildings. Joe Cardona, strolling alone beside the jail, saw the lights come on in

Tharbel's offices. The detective hurried up the stairs. When he arrived in the rear office, he found Scudder and the jailer with Wyngarth in charge.

"You can go back," said Scudder to the jailer. "This man and I will guard the prisoner."

There were no handcuffs on Wyngarth's wrists, but Scudder had a revolver in his hand, and Cardona drew one also. Footsteps sounded on the stairs. Clyde Burke arrived, followed by Joel Neswick.

Cuthbert Challick was the next to appear. He stood with Neswick, in a corner by the door. The windows were open; Cardona was lounging beside one. Burke was in another corner. Scudder had placed Wyngarth by the desk, which was vacant, awaiting the arrival of the prosecutor.

Barry Davies appeared, with a court stenographer. The prosecutor took the seat behind the desk. The stenographer sat on his right, by the rear window where Cardona was stationed.

Hoyt Wyngarth, face buried in hands, was seated at the left of the desk, close to the side window. Scudder, holding his revolver, blocked the door.

Wyngarth raised his head. He seemed very pale. He looked about him; then stared at the prosecutor.

"Where is the dog?" questioned Wyngarth.

"In the front room," broke in Scudder.

"We shall produce the dog later," asserted the prosecutor, in a businesslike tone. "Proceed with your statement. We are ready."

Wyngarth gripped the edge of the desk. Half rising from his chair, he began his story, as he stared steadily at the prosecutor.

"I knew a man named Harlew," he said. "Schuyler Harlew. He was an agent of Mox. He—he knew of things that I had done, and he threatened me—threatened me unless I came to see Mox. I—I did not know where Mox lived. I was brought by Harlew—to do what Mox commanded——"

The stenographer was taking the jerky remarks in shorthand. Wyngarth's facial muscles began to twitch. He gripped the edge of the desk more fiercely. He rose to his feet and clung, stoop-shouldered.

"Mox is a fiend!" gasped Wyngarth. "He is not an old man, as he pretends to be. I have never seen his real face, but I know that his hair and beard are false, because——"

101

"Look out!" The warning came in a quick, firm voice from Cuthbert Challick, who was facing the window. As he uttered the words, the tall inventor sprang forward and shot out his long arms to wrest Hoyt Wyngarth from a point of danger.

The prisoner was paralyzed. Had he been responsive to Challick's instantaneous warning, had he acted with any of the quick instinctiveness that the inventor displayed, Wyngarth might have been saved. His bewildered senses, however, failed him in the crisis.

Just as Cuthbert Challick clutched the prisoner's motionless arm, something whirred through the window and flashed as it struck Wyngarth's back, directly between the shoulders. With a shriek, Wyngarth lost his hold, and twisted sidewise. Challick, with a display of unusual strength, caught the man's body with his right arm, and eased Wyngarth's horror-stricken face forward on the table.

Startled gasps came from every person in the room. Men were on their feet, staring in horror. Cuthbert Challick was gazing downward at the man whose life he had been unable to save.

Hoyt Wyngarth was coughing blood upon the desk. His breath was choking. He was dying. Straight upward from his pitifully bent shoulders projected the weapon that had brought his doom; the quivering rounded handle of a knife that was buried to the hilt in the victim's body.

Death had interrupted the testimony of Hoyt Wyngarth. The doom that Wyngarth feared had been delivered!

CHAPTER XVIII

DEATH RETURNED

Joe Cardona was at the window, peering through the dusk. He was boldly facing the death that had struck down Hoyt Wyngarth.

Like Cuthbert Challick, however, the sleuth was warned. His quick eyes had spotted the object which the inventor had spied just before the knife arrived.

A distorted figure was clambering from a tree on the other side of the vacant lot. Challick had seen it motionless; Cardona spotted the creature more quickly, now that escape had become its lone desire.

Cardona fired. He knew that he had missed. Another burst came from his revolver; a second miss, just as the creature dropped to the ground, with sprawling, spidery limbs. A third shot blazed from the detective's gun.

This was a hit. Cardona had caught the dwarfish figure on the rise. The creature staggered, then began to bound away in long, limping leaps, running parallel to the row of trees.

Cardona swung his revolver as he fired. He loosed all his bullets rapidly but vainly. The range was too difficult for the detective to hit the moving target.

An automobile had pulled up beside the jail. Cardona saw a man leaping from it. Framed in light, Cardona shouted out an order:

"Get the murderer! Capture him! He can't go far! He's wounded!"

Peering through the dusk, Cardona realized that the man from the car was Junius Tharbel. Instead of pursuing the bounding dwarf, the county detective stood stock still, while Cardona shouted in rage. The limping creature was about to get away!

Cardona saw other men dashing from the jail. He shouted for them to take up the pursuit.

It was then that Tharbel acted. He raised a rifle that he was carrying. As the running creature, almost faded in the dusk, leaped a fence a hundred yards away, the county detective quickly fired.

Simultaneously, the long-limbed fugitive collapsed. Tharbel, lowering his rifle, strode toward the office building, gesturing to the men from the jail to indicate that they should bring in the quarry that he had bagged.

Two figures came running from the car to join Tharbel. Less than three minutes later, the county detective stumped into his office, with Hollis Harman and Wade Hosth behind him. Tharbel glowered in rage as he saw the body of Hoyt Wyngarth upon the desk.

"Is this your doing?" he demanded of Cardona. "Why was the prisoner brought from his cell before I arrived? I am in charge of this case—not you, Cardona!"

"I am the one who acted," interposed Barry Davies, as

Cardona scowled back his challenge to Tharbel. "Wyngarth wanted to make a confession. If you had been here, it would have been in your hands."

"A fine botch!" snorted Tharbel, his hatchetlike countenance flushing crimson. "You're over me, Prosecutor Davies, and you had a right to do this. But you made a great mistake. It was my job to get this man's statement."

He swung to the court stenographer and pointed to the notebook which the man had dropped upon the desk.

"Read what you've got!" he ordered.

In a quavering voice, the stenographer obeyed. When he had finished his reading, Tharbel roared like an enraged bull.

"He was stalling you!" he cried. "Making you look like the suckers you are! He was talking about Mox. He knew he was cornered. This man is Mox—a murderer—and you've let him die without learning the truth!"

With a glum expression, Tharbel stared at Wyngarth's dead body. He seized the handle of the knife, and twisted it free from the dead man's back. He looked at the long, sharp-pointed blade; then, with a violent, angry stroke, drove the point deep into the desk beside the body, and left the knife quivering there.

There were calls from below. Tharbel, pacing the floor, swung to the window. The men from the jail were barely visible in the growing dusk. They were carrying a limp object. Tharbel ordered them to bring their burden upstairs.

The office assumed the appearance of a morgue when the twisted body of the ugly drawf was deposited upon the floor. The creature was dead. The men who had picked him up said that he had died in their arms.

"He tried to talk to us," informed one. "He sort of waved his arms and said: 'Mox—Mox'; then he thumped his hands against his chest and said: 'Sulu—Sulu.' After that, he just coughed and died."

"See?" challenged Tharbel, swinging around to look at every member of the silent group. "There's the answer. He meant that he had killed Mox. Then he told his own name. Sulu."

Swinging past Wyngarth's body, the county detective yanked open the desk drawer and brought out the two notes—the one which he had held; the one which had come to Cardona. He pointed to the letter "S" which served as signature on each message.

"That means Sulu," affirmed Tharbel. "It's all plain now. Wyngarth was Mox. Sulu was his servant. Does that knife look like the one that plugged Schuyler Harlew?"

"Exactly," returned Cardona. "But I don't see how it could be thrown that distance——"

Cardona paused as one of the men who had brought in Sulu's body grinned sheepishly. From his hip pocket he drew a short, thick-barreled gun that he had brought back beneath his coat.

"I picked this up side of the fence," said the man. "Shoved it under my coat, and on my hip, so I could help carry the dead guy. Looks like an air gun."

It was an air gun. Cardona saw that the moment that he received the weapon. He pulled the knife from Tharbel's desk and found that the cylindrical handle fitted perfectly in the muzzle of the air gun.

"Now I know how he got Harlew," announced Cardona soberly. "He could have plugged him through the open window, where Harlew was sitting. This gun has a range, and is accurate. We've seen it work."

"Yes," retorted Tharbel sourly. "You've seen it kill Mox."

He pointed to Wyngarth's body as he spoke.

"What about Salbrook?" questioned Cardona. "I brought him in here——"

"I'm going to free Salbrook," interrupted Tharbel testily. "This case is ended. Mox is dead. Put down this statement" —he was turning to the court stenographer—"and you'll have my final conclusions.

"Mox—Jarvis Moxton—was Hoyt Wyngarth in disguise. He had a servant named Sulu, who escaped with him. He probably deserted Sulu, who, to get revenge, put a note under my door, telling where Wyngarth could be found.

"After that, Sulu, to square himself with Mox, tried to make amends by naming Irving Salbrook in another note. Salbrook was probably the former owner of the dog, and Sulu figured that the test with him would get Wyngarth free.

"When that didn't work, Sulu became afraid. He watched the jail, and when he saw Wyngarth—Mox—brought up here, he decided to kill him before he could name Sulu as the murderer of Schuyler Harlew."

"How about questioning Salbrook?" asked Cardona, when Tharbel had completed his statement. "He can tell us whether or not he once owned the dog that——"

"You've let the real crook die!" interrupted Tharbel hotly. "Wyngarth is the one I wanted to question. He was the prisoner I landed. You brought Irving Salbrook here; you can take him away."

"I've got no charge against him," declared Cardona. "I was after the man who killed Schuyler Harlew. Here he is"—Cardona pointed to Sulu—"and that ends it for me."

"Then release Salbrook after I turn him back to you. I intend to question him in my own way. I'll tell him what has happened; if he wants to talk, he can. If he wants to keep mum, he'll go out of my jail in the morning."

Tharbel turned toward the county prosecutor, and glared as he spoke. Barry Davies, realizing that his own use of authority had ruined Tharbel's plans, made no objection. Cardona, however, was still bitter in his protest.

"Maybe I helped lead Wyngarth to his death," said Cardona, "but I didn't kill Sulu. I wounded him—that's all. You're the one who killed him, Tharbel, when you didn't have to kill him."

"Then we're quits," glowered Tharbel. "You killed my suspect; I killed yours."

Assuming his show of authority, Tharbel waved toward the bodies as he spoke to Scudder and the men from the jail.

"This is no morgue," he said testily. "Get these corpses out of here. Then clean the place up. Take them in here."

Opening the door ahead, Tharbel stepped into the lighted front room. As he disappeared from view, the others heard an angry exclamation come from his lips; then came the sound of joyous yelps. Tharbel came retreating through the door, the brown-spotted Dalmatian leaping upon him as a dog that has found its master.

"Who brought the hound here?" shouted Tharbel, as he cuffed the dog. "Take him away from me! Take him away!"

The coach dog did not seem to mind the blows that Tharbel was delivering. Clyde Burke leaped forward and grabbed the dog's collar. The Dalmatian snarled fiercely. It broke away madly.

Cuthbert Challick seized the beast by the collar. He swung it about, and began to pull and drag it toward the front room.

Under this treatment, the Dalmatian cowered. It lost its fight, and whined as Challick pushed it into the front room. Slinking, the dog went to a far corner and lay quiet.

As Challick stepped aside, the men carried the first of the two bodies past. Clyde Burke was nursing scratches that he had gained in his struggle with the dog. Junius Tharbel was striding about the room in ruffled fashion.

"That settles it," he blurted. "The fact that the dog made friends with Irving Salbrook doesn't mean a thing, now that this has happened. I doubt if Salbrook ever saw the dog before."

The men had come back for Wyngarth's body. Tharbel pointed as they carried the dead form into the front room.

"There goes Mox," decided the county detective. "He was the first person the dog liked. After that, it was ready to make friends."

"But with very few people," rejoined Cardona, in an artful tone.

"What's that?" Tharbel caught up the statement. "Hm-m-m. Next thing we know"—he was laughing sullenly—"you'll be asking me to arrest myself."

The county detective swung to the prosecutor. His tone still showed the anger which he had ceased to suppress. Tharbel's customary reserve had disappeared.

"You started this," he told the prosecutor. "Go ahead and finish it. You have my summary. Improve it if you can. Get the coroner for the inquest on those dead men. Plenty of witnesses saw what happened. I'm tired of this interference, and I'm glad the case is over. I'm going out to the hunting lodge, and have a real day's shoot tomorrow. There won't be anyone chasing after me to bring me in here.

"I'll be in to-morrow evening—at my home. If there's anything that turns up, I can take care of it after that time. That settles everything."

Thinking deeply as he listened to Tharbel's dictatorial words, Joe Cardona was staring at the floor. His eyes were upon a blackened silhouette that seemed rooted to the spot where it lay. That splotch was bringing back recollections.

"Do what you want with the dog," Tharbel was adding from the door. "He's a keen animal. He liked me today because I had been out with the dogs since daybreak. If nobody else wants him, we can give him to Harman to keep around the lodge."

Cardona turned to see what reply the prosecutor intended to make. There was none. Swinging back, Cardona noticed that Cuthbert Challick had closed the door to the front room, and was strolling away from it.

Tharbel was leaving. Hollis Harman, the jovial-faced fellow, was going with him. So was Wade Hosth, the tall, solemn huntsman. Neither of Tharbel's companions made a comment.

"What are you going to do about it?" queried Cardona, of the prosecutor.

"Follow Tharbel's suggestions," replied Davies. "He's the county detective—not I. This piece of machinery"—he tapped the air gun—"will be yours after the inquests."

"I'm going over to the inn," remarked Cuthbert Challick, from the door by the hall. "I'll have dinner with you, later on."

"All right," agreed Cardona.

After Challick had started down the stairs, Cardona suddenly remembered the spot on the floor. He glanced hastily about him; besides the prosecutor and the stenographer, there were only three others in the room. Clyde Burke, Joel Neswick, and Scudder had remained where they were.

Then Cardona looked to the floor. The silhouette was gone. A thoughtful expression appeared upon the detective's swarthy face. He was positive now that the case was not closed. New angles lay ahead.

Hoyt Wyngarth was not Mox. The man had been too frightened, too sincere, to be the master fiend. Mox still lived; the villain could yet wreak mischief. Sulu, the murderous minion, was dead. Whatever malice Mox contemplated would have to be of his own doing.

Hoyt Wyngarth was dead because he had talked too much. Danger, perhaps, faced Irving Salbrook if he should dare to speak. Cardona saw the possibilities that lay ahead, however. Salbrook might be valuable, once Mox was brought to bay.

That was the game: to uncover Mox himself! While Salbrook still remained a prisoner, the master plotter would never travel far from Darport.

Uncover Mox? How could it be done?

The answer lay in the profiled shadow which Cardona

had spotted on the floor. The ace detective had failed to note the man whom that silhouette represented, but he had a hunch as to who its owner was.

With The Shadow still in Darport, there would be a chance to corner Mox. That was the game that Cardona meant to play. In the back of his head, the star detective saw the way.

He had confidence—Cardona—now that he had seen the mystic profile. For that splotch of facial blackness was a token that Cardona had seen before.

Cardona had recognized the silhouette as the sign of The Shadow's presence. Here, in this room, The Shadow had viewed double death, and had witnessed the events which followed it.

The Shadow, like Joe Cardona, would be ready to end the evil career of Mox. With such an ally close at hand, Cardona felt that he could win the grim game!

CHAPTER XIX

CARDONA'S PLAN

Joe Cardona stayed at the Darport Inn that night. So did Joel Neswick, Cuthbert Challick, and Clyde Burke. The four were to testify at the coroner's inquests the next day.

They formed a friendly group, these four: two inventors, a reporter, and a detective. All the while, Joe Cardona maintained his thoughts. His plan was formulating hour by hour.

When the inquests ended the next day, and the four men returned to the inn to pack up, the time had come for Cardona to begin his action.

There was a subtle message which Cardona intended to convey. Because of the friendship which he had formed with his three companions, he decided to confide with them in a group. At the inn, he found Challick in the lobby, and signaled the inventor to come with him. In an upstairs room, he discovered Neswick packing. Clyde Burke was there, chatting with the second inventor.

Cardona closed the door. He made a dramatic gesture,

109

and his companions turned in his direction. Neswick stopped packing. Cardona began to talk.

"What I've got to say is confidential," he declared. "That applies to you in particular, Burke. I know you well enough. You're too smart a reporter to kill a story before it breaks."

"Spill it, Joe," suggested Clyde.

"I am convinced," declared Cardona firmly, "that Hoyt Wyngarth was not Mox."

Looks of surprise came from the other men.

"Who do you suspect, Joe?" quizzed Clyde. "Irving Salbrook?"

"No." Cardona shook his head. "I'm not naming anybody. I've just got a general sort of hunch—that's all. Do you want to hear it?"

"Sure thing."

"First of all," asserted Cardona, "Mox had his agent, Schuyler Harlew. He was the fellow who kidded you, Neswick, and you, Challick. Mox had a bunch of henchmen, too, a regular mob, in that old house of his. One of the crew was this mug Sulu.

"I think Mox killed Peter Greerson and others, too. Anyway, there was some hook-up between him and both Wyngarth and Salbrook—enough to let him heave the blame on one or the other of them when the crash came. That's just what he did—lay it on Wyngarth, by means of that note that Junius Tharbel showed us."

"But what about the note you got?" queried Burke.

"Somebody planted it in my pocket," announced Cardona. "Somebody must have seen Tharbel's note, and copied it. There's a mysterious figure in this game—a fighter that's out to get Mox. He's the one who rescued you, Neswick. He brought Salbrook into the picture just to kill Mox's plot against Wyngarth.

"I'll tell you what Mox did. He had Sulu bump off Wyngarth. He had the dwarf ready on the job for just what happened. He was hoping that the case could be closed by Wyngarth's death. It was."

"Why don't you quiz Salbrook?" suggested Burke.

"Because Mox would try to get him if I did," returned Cardona. "If Salbrook goes free and keeps mum, he'll be all right. It's a lucky break for him, the way things have turned out."

"But if Mox came after Irving Salbrook——"

"I know; I could be there to try and save him. But I

110

didn't save Wyngarth, did I? You weren't even able to do that, Challick"—Cardona spoke approvingly—"although you made a great attempt to do so when you spotted Sulu in the tree.

"No, sir. This time, Mox would try the job himself. Even in New York, Salbrook wouldn't be safe. He wouldn't talk in New York; he wouldn't have to. We've got no charge against him there, outside of some petty racketeering.

"But I've figured a way to make Salbrook talk. That's to meet Mox myself. Maybe I won't be alone. Maybe The—the hidden player will be in the game, too. But here's how I'm going to work it. The State police have left that old house."

"I see," observed Challick, with a slight smile. "You believe in the old theory of a murderer returning to the scene of his crime."

"Bunk, as a rule," returned Cardona. "But not if the murderer knows that there's a chance for another murder awaiting him!"

Eyebrows raised. Cardona's scheme was just beginning to make itself apparent. The detective continued.

"Mox murdered at midnight," he declared. "I'll bet the fox still can get in and out of that house without being seen. So I'm going over there to-night. Going alone, understand. You two will be out of town"—he nodded toward Neswick and then Challick—"and you'll stay out of the thing, Burke. Understand?"

"All right, Joe. I'll keep away from the old house."

"When I get there," resumed Cardona, "I'll meet Mox. I'll get him; he won't get me. We'll find out who Mox is, after I'm through with him."

"But how," questioned Challick thoughtfully, "can you give Mox the idea that you'll be there?"

"Leave that to me," laughed Cardona. "He'll find out quick enough, if he's anywhere around. I've spoken in confidence. Don't say anything to anyone. There's only one other whom I intend to see about this matter."

"Junius Tharbel?" questioned Clyde Burke.

"Yes," replied Cardona. "I'll speak to him when he shows up from the hunting lodge. He's due in this evening. I'll get his permission to visit the old house. Just a matter of formality, you know. Courtesy."

"Suppose he refuses?"

"He won't."

"Maybe he'll want to go with you."

"Not a chance. He'll laugh at me. But I'll have the last laugh before I'm through."

"Cardona," said Neswick seriously, "I'm going out on the next train. I'll have to hurry to make it. I'm glad you told me about this. Do you actually know who Mox is?"

"I ought to know," returned Cardona wisely. "I'm a detective. Sometimes very obvious things escape notice. Some detectives are not logical. Take Tharbel, for instance. He figured the dog test was great stuff at first; afterward, he said it was only good when it worked with Hoyt Wyngarth."

Clyde Burke's lips parted. The reporter restrained the words that he was about to utter. Instead, he turned to both Neswick and Challick.

"Cardona is a keen fellow," he explained, "and he has tact. I see his point. It doesn't do to throw accusations—particularly when they involve a person of importance. We'll let the matter rest for a while. Wait until he meets Mox."

Neswick nodded and went back to his packing. Challick strolled from the room. He spoke to Cardona after he had passed the door.

"I expect to take the evening train," he said. "We can dine together—you and I and Burke."

"All right," agreed Cardona, "but mum will be the word from now on."

"Absolutely."

Neswick took his early train. Challick and Burke joined Cardona at dinner. Afterward, the inventor went up to pack. Burke offered to drive him to the station in the coupé. Challick thanked him, but said that he had already summoned a cab.

After Challick's departure, Cardona said that he intended to call on Tharbel. Burke offered to drive him there. This invitation was accepted. They reached Tharbel's house, and went in to see the county detective.

Tharbel seemed rather surprised to see the visitors. His hatchet face hardened. Nevertheless, he assumed a friendly attitude.

"Thought that you fellows would be gone," he said, "now that this Mox business is ended."

"It's not ended," returned Cardona seriously. "I believe that we've missed an important bet. The old house."

"It's been searched from top to bottom!" exclaimed Tharbel. "You saw the secret rooms that we uncovered. This is a ridiculous idea, Cardona."

"The house is unguarded now," affirmed Cardona. "I want to be there at midnight."

"You don't believe that Wyngarth was Mox?"

"I'm not saying that," returned Cardona, wisely appeasing Tharbel's wrath. "I just figured that there may be something we don't know about. Maybe the answer can be found at midnight—when the place is empty."

"You're crazy," decided Tharbel.

"Maybe," said Cardona calmly. "Just the same, I'd like to go there. I'm here to ask your permission to do so."

"Is that all? Go right ahead. Maybe you'll find some spooks in the place. Take a look upstairs. Go through the place all you want."

"Thanks," said Cardona, rising. "How was the hunting?"

"Punk," growled Tharbel. "Fatty Harman wants me to come back again to-morrow, but I guess I've had enough. Wade Hosth pulled out this afternoon, too. Say—just a minute. Are you taking Burke along with you to-night?"

"No."

"All right, then. You can go to the place, as a police officer. The risk is yours. But I don't want any reporters or others around the place. The State troopers might just happen to drop in for a final inspection. Your badge will make it all right for you, but the State police are strict, and it might mean trouble for anyone else."

Joe Cardona and Clyde Burke departed. The reporter was thoughtful as they rode back to the inn. He had called Burbank before dinner. He had received instructions to be on hand at the inn. Clyde wanted to be alone in case of another call.

"Think I'll nap to midnight," remarked Cardona. It was just the break that Clyde Burke wanted. "I've got an alarm clock, and I'll set it for quarter of twelve. I'll walk to the old house, Burke. Remember—you're out of this."

"I'm not going there," Clyde assured the detective. "I'll be turning in by nine o'clock myself."

It was nine when the two reached the Darport Inn. They parted, and each man went to his room. The two were located on the third floor.

Joe Cardona smiled as he set his alarm clock for quarter

of twelve. He placed the clock beside the bed, and lay down to think. He was ready for to-night's adventure.

For Joe Cardona's hunch was working to perfection. He was positive that he knew how matters lay. His conversations, first with Burke and the inventors; second, with Junius Tharbel had been delivered with a subtle purpose.

Joe Cardona knew that his intentions for to-night had certainly reached two persons. One was The Shadow. The other was Mox. Joe had arranged his actions so that both would know; and he was sure that he had succeeded.

At midnight, Cardona reflected, he would keep an unscheduled appointment with the murderer, Mox. When the fatal hour struck, The Shadow would be there!

CHAPTER XX

BEFORE MIDNIGHT

It was half past nine. The telephone bell rang in Clyde Burke's room. The reporter answered it promptly. He spoke his name into the mouthpiece. The voice that came through the receiver brought a chill to his spine, so sinister was its whisper.

"Report."

Tensely, Clyde Burke told of the visit that he and Joe Cardona had paid to Junius Tharbel's home. Clyde had already reported to Burbank the conversation that had taken place in Joel Neswick's room, when Cuthbert Challick was also present.

"Instructions."

Clyde Burke listened intently.

"Blink lights in your own room to signal Cardona's departure," came The Shadow's voice. "Once. If departure is delayed, twice. If you should discover Cardona gone, three times."

The receiver clicked at the other end. Clyde Burke knew that the call had been a local one. The Shadow was somewhere close at hand.

The instructions concerning the blinking of the lights were merely an indication of The Shadow's thoroughness.

Clyde Burke was sure that Cardona's alarm clock would give him the news that the detective had awakened. After that, he would surely see the detective leave.

Enfolding night had wrapped its inky blackness over Darport. Away from the town lights, the old house of Mox stood silent and deserted. Yet it did not lack a living presence. An hour after Clyde Burke had received The Shadow's call, a strange figure crept noiselessly into the shelter of the old building.

Up to the roof of the shed, then to the roof of the house. There was no moon. The Shadow's ascending form did not even make a moving splotch. There was no hesitation in The Shadow's climb. The ascent was easy, and there was no easing of the left arm, which had now regained its full strength.

The Shadow stopped by the large chimney. Wind whistled about his cloak. Rising to the top of the chimney, The Shadow moved downward into the chimney itself. His foot and hands found ladderlike niches. He descended.

The perpendicular passage came to an ending. The Shadow's flashlight revealed the interior of a fireplace; but there was no opening at the front—the bottom of the shaft was solid on all four sides.

The Shadow's gloved right hand twisted a lever that projected within the chimney. The wall in front of him began to move downward. Then came an opening—with light. The floor of an illuminated room came into view, and settled on a level with the bottom of the fireplace.

The Shadow had produced Mox's secret lair, with all its furniture and decorations!

The Shadow stepped into the lighted room. He laughed. The low desk, the short-backed chairs, the small bookcases; all these were part of the scheme. Only The Shadow had managed to uncover the ingenious secret of Mox!

The two secret rooms which the police had discovered were dummies. The wall between them was thick; it moved up and down within a hollow wall below. It was actually the plunger of an elevator, operated by mechanism in a sub-basement which had no entrance except the small shaft that ran straight down through the movable wall at the spot where the anteroom was located.

The anteroom was part of the large room. Its pit was funnel-shaped, to give thickness to the wall beneath it. The victims who had plunged to doom had gone into a smooth-sided vortex—a hollow, inverted cone—that took them like a trap catches helpless flies.

Leaving or entering, by the fireplace, Mox had only to press the lever, and his secret room would rise beneath the attic, forming two smaller—and lower—rooms beneath. When up, the center wall—the plunger of the elevator—blocked both fireplace and panel in the hallway.

The panels on each side of the central one were mechanically blocked by a short, ledgelike inner wall when the furnished room was down. When the room was up, there was still sufficient space for the low ledge and the furniture.

It was the lowness of the ceilings in the dummy rooms that had given The Shadow the clew to something above. He had entered the chimney the night of his investigation, and had found the secret room.

The Shadow opened the drawer of Mox's desk. There he found cards intact. These contained the names and histories of victims. They also gave information regarding Hoyt Wyngarth and Irving Salbrook; facts which told The Shadow of their connection with Mox.

Thousands of dollars were in the desk drawer. It was for the cash that Sulu had tried to enter the house at Mox's bidding. The dwarf had failed to pass the police cordon. Well did The Shadow know that Mox himself would return now that the police were gone!

The Shadow moved swiftly across the room and raised the inner panel of the anteroom. Clanking sounds announced work that he was doing; the blackness of his cloak obscured his actual motions. When The Shadow arose and turned away, no change was apparent. The laugh of The Shadow echoed weirdly from the walls of Mox's secret room!

Back to the fireplace went The Shadow. His form entered the opening; his hand pressed the lever. The secret room began to rise; not even the slightest sound of mechanism was audible. The lifting apparatus was muffled in the subcellar far beneath the house.

Out from the chimney; down the roof; the shed; and then the ground. The shape of The Shadow had blended with the darkness of night. The master sleuth did not intend to await the coming of Mox. He had chosen to find the fiend within the lair.

A blotch of blackness passed beneath the illumination of

a street lamp near Junius Tharbel's home. The county detective's house was dark. Everyone had apparently gone to bed.

On went The Shadow, like a silent ghost of the night air. He stopped at a distance from the Darport Inn. There, he watched the lighted window that indicated Clyde Burke's room.

It was nearing midnight. Clyde Burke, watch in hand, noted the time at fifteen minutes before the hour. He wondered about Cardona's alarm clock. The reporter opened the door of his room. He heard the alarm clock begin to ring.

The sound was intermittent. A short ring, then silence; after that a repeat. When three rings had occurred, Clyde realized that Cardona should have turned off the clock. The fourth ring came as Clyde stole along the hall.

The reporter, sensing something wrong, knocked upon the door. There was no response. Clyde seized the top of the door frame, got his foot on the knob, and raised himself to peer through the transom. The room was empty!

Joe Cardona had evidently awakened before quarter of twelve, and had gone out quietly. He had left a light burning in the corner; he had forgotten to push the silencer of the alarm clock.

Dully, Clyde Burke realized that he had failed in an important duty. Cardona's life might be at stake! Then the reporter remembered the emergency instructions of The Shadow. Dashing back to his own room, he turned off the light and paused. Then, rapidly, he turned the light on and off three times in quick succession.

In the outer darkness, The Shadow saw the signal. His laugh was a grim whisper in the cool night air. The Shadow understood. Joe Cardona was already on his way to keep his arranged appointment with Mox, the murderer.

Swiftly, silently, The Shadow swept away through the night, taking the trail which he knew the detective must have followed. The Shadow was on his way to save Cardona from Mox, the super-fiend. There was time—for Mox had the hour at which he preferred to strike.

Death was due at midnight. The Shadow would arrive before the fatal hour! It would be his task to stay the fiendish hand of Mox, the monster, should Joe Cardona fail.

117

Joe Cardona's beliefs were vague. The Shadow's knowledge was complete. At midnight, Mox, the murderer, would stand revealed.

The Shadow knew!

CHAPTER XXI

THE FATAL HOUR

Joe Cardona was entering the old house at almost the exact minute when Clyde Burke's signal had reached The Shadow. The detective was carrying a flashlight. He flickered its rays through the downstairs hall.

Three figures arose as one. Before the sleuth could use his revolver, his enemies were upon him. They muffled the detective's cries. They threatened him with revolver butts unless he maintained complete silence. Joe Cardona subsided.

The detective's own handcuffs clicked upon his wrists. Joe's hands were behind his back. His keys remained in his vest pocket. He could not reach them. Gruff voices told him that his captors must be gangsters.

By the glow of flashlights, Joe was led upstairs. One of his captors stopped at the center panel in the upper corridor. He raised it. Joe Cardona was unceremoniously thrust into the little anteroom.

The panel clicked behind him. Silence followed. Joe could not hear the trudge of the gangsters who were going downstairs again.

A click. Up came the barring panel in front. Joe Cardona staggered into the lighted room. He stopped, bewildered, as he faced the man with stooped shoulders, gray hair and beard, who sat behind the table, his eyes glittering evilly at Cardona.

The detective could see that the make-up was false, when viewed from close range. With anger on his face, Cardona looked squarely at this fiend, who chose to hide his own countenance under the false guise of Mox.

"So! The word was followed by Mox's cackled laugh.

"You have come to see me, eh? That is good. Very good."

Cardona remained silent. He knew that the voice, like the face, was a pretense. He could see the clock above Mox's head. It showed the time as being eight minutes before twelve o'clock.

"You like my den?" Mox was chuckling with sarcasm. "Others have liked it, before you. All of them have died. But not as you will die. I have reserved for you the keeping of my secret room—for to-night is my last visit here."

Mox paused; then he began an explanation as he surveyed Cardona narrowly.

"This room," he cackled, "is an elevator. It goes up, but it leaves a space, for the lever in the chimney stops it at a certain point.

"To-night, after I depart, I shall break that lever free. I have already loosened it. The floor of this room will go up. It will not stop. Furniture—everything—will be crushed—and Joe Cardona with it!"

Mox flourished a revolver as he spoke. There was no chance for Joe Cardona to escape the monster. With one hand, Mox piled stacks of money on the desk, chuckling as he did.

"I came for this," he laughed. "Wealth, with which I lured inventors to their doom. The inventors are at the bottom of my pit—there in the anteroom. I have their inventions; through proxies, I can release them.

"You thought my henchmen were all slain. They were; but I had others available. Gangsters, in New York. I called them to-night, after you had told me of your plans. They were here to greet you. They are waiting below—until after midnight."

The hands of the clock were almost at the fatal hour. Mox arose from his desk and approached Cardona. Holding the gun in his hand, he sneered at the detective and emitted his cackled laugh. His eyes were on Cardona's face. They noticed nothing else.

"You shall die!" chuckled Mox. "Die because you tried to thwart me. Irving Salbrook will be freed—the only man who could tell anything—and he, like Hoyt Wyngarth, never learned enough to injure me."

"I learned plenty!" growled Joe Cardona. "I saw your game. I got the final hunch when I watched the dog. It

119

betrayed you. If you had made a real slip, I would have denounced you then. I know you, in spite of your false beard and hair, and your crazy voice."

"Then I shall not remove my disguise," laughed Mox. "Since you know me, you do not have to see my real face again."

"A clever game." Joe was defiant. "To play the part of a man opposed to crime, and secretly commit murders of your own. Kill me, if you want—but remember—one man, at least, found out your true identity. You murderer!"

The clock was at the point of twelve. Mox chuckled. He bowed. He nudged his free hand toward the fireplace. He was about to announce his departure.

"I must inconvenience you," he cackled, "by showing you how hard my fist can strike. That will be easy, since your hands are cuffed. You will not follow me to safety."

Scornfully, Joe Cardona thrust out his jaw. Mox clenched his fist. Its sinews showed the strength of this pretended old man. But before the blow came, Cardona hurled his last defiance.

"I know you!" he cried. "I know you! My last act shall be to shout out your name even though no one may hear me. I know you! Junius Tharbel!"

As the name spat from Cardona's lips, Mox replied with a hoarse, crackling laugh. His left fist swung up and clipped the detective's chin. Joe Cardona staggered and fell down to the floor.

Junius Tharbel!

The accusing name seemed to echo as Mox turned chuckling to seize the money from the desk. Joe Cardona had played his hunch. He had used Tharbel's own system. When the dog had made its happy leap for the county detective, Joe had gained the answer that he wanted. He had picked Tharbel as the dog's real master.

A click resounded from the other side of the room. The noise audible despite the fatal striking of the clock, caused Mox to turn. There, in the anteroom, Mox saw The Shadow! Like a being from another world, the master had arrived to arrest the monster's flight!

Mox did not falter. Even the sight of the threatening automatic in The Shadow's hand did not deter him. The fiend's hand was upon the desk. Instead of the pile of wealth, it chose the button that was close by.

With a cackling cry, this fiend whom Cardona had

denounced as Junius Tharbel pressed the button. His action was answered by the sound of the opening trap. With eyes upon the button, Mox cackled. He was sending The Shadow down the shaft of doom!

CHAPTER XXII

DOOM DEFERRED

A laugh from the anteroom was the answer to Mox's pressure of the button. Looking up, the disguised villain gasped. The Shadow had not dropped with the falling of the trap. He was standing, apparently in air, within the anteroom!

As Mox stooped, rigid, The Shadow spoke. His words began just as the chimes had ceased their striking. The fatal hour of twelve had passed. Mox had not delivered death at midnight.

"I remain," declared The Shadow, in an ominous whisper. "Your trap fell, but without its burden. I have been here before you, Mox."

Staring, Mox saw now why The Shadow had not dropped through the opened trap. The being in black was standing on two steel rods that had been fitted across the floor of the anteroom. That was the work which The Shadow had done on his visit before midnight.

"I surprised your henchmen," sneered The Shadow, "as easily as they surprised Cardona. Shots from this floor might be heard. Those downstairs were not."

Slowly, The Shadow advanced across the room. He avoided Cardona, who was lying groggy, on the floor, and stood face to face with Mox.

"Your game was plain," came The Shadow's mocking tone. "I found your records—on my first visit here. You did not have your own name marked. Wyngarth and Salbrook were ones that I discovered.

"They were not victims; nor henchmen. They were dupes, who feared you because you knew too much about them. There were times when you were forced to be away.

121

You needed someone to play the part of Mox—to stay in your living room—guised as an old man.

"Such dupes would be useful, later on, to mark as Mox. You had two in order to be safe. Hoyt Wyngarth and Irving Salbrook. They lived here in turns. They went outside—always guarded. Thus Jarvis Moxton was seen around his home even when you were away."

Mox snarled. His chuckle was forgotten. The Shadow had told him the truth.

"You sent Sulu to kill Harlew," resumed The Shadow, in a taunting tone. "Your note, written in Sulu's scrawl, was duplicated by my hand. Two men brought in their suspects. Joe Cardona matched Junius Tharbel's measure.

"Sulu was ready to kill Hoyt Wyngarth. He succeeded. Although I was watching affairs, guised as a stranger in Darport, I did not prevent that death. Wyngarth's foolish desire to tell his story was something unexpected.

"I suspected you from the time I saw you. But your betrayal came at the time you least expected it. Then I was sure that you were Mox. Your dog betrayed you!

"The dog liked Wyngarth. He had made friends with it. Disguise means nothing to a dog. It recognized Hoyt Wyngarth as a master. Irving Salbrook, too, when he played the part of Mox, was friendly to the dog. It recognized him as a master that it also loved.

"But when the dog came to Junius Tharbel!" The Shadow's laugh came now as a weird, taunting whisper. "That was different. That was chance. Tharbel had been with dogs all day. Of course, it was natural that another dog should come to him!"

Joe Cardona was sitting up. Although half groggy, he was drinking in The Shadow's words. He saw the tall form that dominated the cowering figure of Mox. He heard the name of Junius Tharbel as The Shadow uttered it.

"You"—The Shadow's eyes were blazing upon the fiend before him—"were the dog's real master. It should act toward you as toward no one else. It did act so!

"You, a fiend with no human kindness in your evil heart, could never win the love of even a dog! That is why I learned your identity—when the dog cowered and crawled away as it recognized the man whose evil wrath it feared. That is how I came to know you for Mox, Cuthbert Challick!"

The Shadow's free hand shot forward and ripped the hair

and beard from the monster's face. Joe Cardona, staring, gasped in amazement as he recognized the features of the man whom The Shadow had named—Cuthbert Challick!

The truth was plain. Challick had posed as a future victim of Mox, the murderer. He had come boldly to Joe Cardona. He had given testimony to support Joel Neswick. He had signaled to Sulu to slay Hoyt Wyngarth. His effort to save the doomed man had been a dramatic pretense.

Joe Cardona, still half dazed, groped amid his errors. Pride, not falsity, had governed Junius Tharbel. The county detective had slain Sulu not to get rid of a wounded henchman, as Cardona had thought, but to actually stop a fleeing murderer. His explanation of the dog's friendliness had been correct.

But Cuthbert Challick! Cardona understood. The cowering of the slinking dog, its immediate retirement to a corner; those were the signs of a real but brutal master. The dog had growled at others, but not at Cuthbert Challick!

Tense seconds had passed, then came the counter move. It was so rapid that Cardona did not realize what happened until the action was finished. With a fiendish snarl, Cuthbert Challick snapped his right hand from beneath the table edge, swinging his revolver directly toward The Shadow.

A roar resounded through the secret room. Quick though Challick was, he could not match his hand swing against the finger pressure of The Shadow. The burst of flame that accompanied the roar was delivered from the muzzle of The Shadow's automatic. Cuthbert Challick sprawled upon the desk; then rolled to the floor and lay still. He had made his last move.

The Shadow turned to Joe Cardona. The detective was half seated, with his hands propping his body behind him. A black glove whisked from The Shadow's left hand. Cardona stared, fascinated, as he viewed the gleaming girasol on The Shadow's finger.

The jewel went from sight as The Shadow brought the keys from Cardona's vest. Stooping, the being in black released the detective's wrists. Cardona staggered to his feet. He made his way toward the anteroom, with its open panel. The path was safe; the trap had risen automatically.

Cardona pressed the outer panel and found that it opened readily from the inside. He turned as he reached the corridor, holding the panel open. He stared as he saw The

Shadow stooping within the fireplace. The lever clattered to the hearth. The Shadow laughed with bursting triumph. The floor of the secret room began to rise.

The wall blocked Cardona's view. It kept moving up—up—up—until a crunching of woodwork and ruined furniture told of the finale which Mox had planned. Mox the superfiend was already dead. And now his body was crushed.

Thus came the end of Cuthbert Challick, the inventor who had sought wealth through the murder of men whose plans he stole.

Joe Cardona let the panel fall. He went downstairs. He passed the bodies of the gunmen whom The Shadow had conquered in a swift, fair fray—a lone hand against three. The cool air of night was reviving to Joe Cardona.

As the detective paused, breathing deeply, he heard a weird sound that came as a ghostly cry from the summit of the old house. The sibilant tones of a sinister laugh swept forth in triumphant merriment.

The triumph laugh of The Shadow! The victorious cry of the superbeing who had deferred the stroke of doom!

It was The Shadow's knell above the tomb of Mox!

CHAPTER XXIII

CARDONA LEARNS

Joe Cardona aroused Junius Tharbel that very night. He told his story of his visit to the house of Mox, but he said nothing of the identity of the mysterious stranger who had helped him. Joe claimed to have been groggy all the while.

Junius Tharbel listened, but the county detective held his doubts. The morrow, however, produced the evidence. Cardona demanded an investigation of the chimney. The shaft was explored. The loose lever was replaced. The real secret room was brought down.

The broken body of Cuthbert Challick was discovered. Thousands of dollars in currency was recovered from the room. Records were taken from broken drawers and book cases. The full details of Mox's schemes were learned.

Investigation of the death pit enabled Cardona and Tharbel to uncover the bodies of those whom Mox had sent to doom. Peter Greerson and six other inventors were identified.

Irving Salbrook, when he learned of the death of Mox, told how he had lived at the house guised as the old man when Cuthbert Challick had been absent. He had not known of the secret room, but he, like Hoyt Wyngarth, had been intimidated by the fiend.

Sulu had used the cupboard to keep watch on Salbrook during his stays at the house. The death of Schuyler Harlew had broken Salbrook's nerve. He, like Hoyt Wyngarth, had been afraid to speak.

To Joe Cardona, however, one important fact remained unsolved. The star detective admitted—to himself, alone—that he had been grievously mistaken. He had built up a case against Junius Tharbel, and had thought that the county detective was Mox; but, worse than that, Cardona had been positive that Cuthbert Challick was The Shadow!

That was why he had discussed his plans in Challick's presence. He had tried to inform The Shadow; his visit to Tharbel's had been to inform Mox! Cardona did not know how The Shadow had really learned of what was in the air. He did not suspect that Clyde Burke was The Shadow's agent.

Joe Cardona remained in Darport for several days, and all the while he still wondered. He remembered the note placed in his pocket; the profile on the floor of Tharbel's office. He puzzled over the problem of The Shadow's identity during the progress of this case.

The day before his departure from Darport, Cardona accompanied Junius Tharbel on a trip to Hollis Harman's hunting lodge. Cardona and Tharbel were now the best of friends. Harman, a smile on his pudgy face, welcomed them into his place.

"Note from a friend of yours, Cardona," remarked Harman. "Congratulations, I suppose, on your great work in this case."

Cardona stared as he opened the envelope which Harman gave him. Inside, he found a brief note, with it, a calling card. The note was a brief congratulation; its writing faded mysteriously as Joe Cardona finished reading it.

Cardona looked at the card. He stared blankly. He read the name more closely:

WADE HOSTH

Harman's friend at the lodge! The extra huntsman who had been with Junius Tharbel so often during the days when Mox had been sought. The silent man who had watched everything, but who had said nothing!

The Dalmatian, stretched beside the hearth, looked up as Cardona sat down near it. The dog was friendly to strangers now. It had been adopted by Junius Tharbel. The county detective was keeping it at Harman's lodge.

Joe Cardona did not notice the dog. His eyes were on the card in his hand. The light began to dawn. Drawing a pencil from his pocket, Joe Cardona marked down the fourth letter of Wade Hosth's last name. Then the last letter of the last name; the last letter of the first.

A space. Cardona put down an S, the middle letter of Hosth; then the first letter of the same name. He followed by placing the other letters, until his task was complete.

Letter for letter, a perfect anagram, the name of Wade Hosth declared the title of the superman who had used that pseudonym to answer for the identity which he had assumed.

There, in Cardona's own printing, appeared the name of the mighty being who had ended the insidious career of Mox. Cardona read it with silent, moving lips:

THE SHADOW.